The Doleful Petal

MEHNOOR HAYATH

Clever Fox®
PUBLISHING
Chennai • Bangalore

CLEVER FOX PUBLISHING
Chennai, India

Published by CLEVER FOX PUBLISHING 2025

ISBN: 978-93-6707-226-4

Blurb

An orphan takes care of another orphan, his own age. He finds her unique—different from everyone else. He senses that there's something special in her, something that could one day protect their future. He devotes himself to her so deeply that he ends up destroying an entire unknown kingdom for her.

She, who never belonged to a normal family, struggles to trust the boy who raised her. She always suspects that he knows almost everything about her childhood. As she grew older, she discovers something she wishes she hadn't. But to reveal it, she is willing to do whatever it takes.

Contents

1. Why You Must Learn Morse Codes 1

2. Gladious 12

3. Lily 27

4. Oleander 43

5. Chrysanthemums 55

6. Diphylleia Grayi Flower 73

7. Droghego 91

Chapter 1

Why You Must Learn Morse Codes

He leaned against a tree, sat down, and opened a book.

'It was a sunny day; my mom was giving me lessons with a warm smile on her face. "You must grow up to become a great warrior, promise me?" Her voice as gentle as the cold summer breeze but determined. "I will, and I promise, mummy!" My little determined words formed a gentle smile on her face, which eventually became an embrace. Just before my mother could break the embrace, a knock was heard; I ran and saw my father bringing in groceries. "Welcome back, father. I suppose you're tired after running the errand; please come in and have a seat." My mom then signalled me to go upstairs; I obeyed her and climbed the stairs. While climbing, I felt an unsettling feeling about something. My mother and father never used to get along with each other; they fought every day, and my mom had scars and bruises all over her face. The fact that I knew yet acted like

I didn't was quite a task for me as a child. 'Ahhh!' A scream was heard; I then ran downstairs to find my father, holding a knife covered with blood. And my mom with a wound on her stomach. She clenched her stomach and shouted at my father, "You—you monster! What about your unborn child! Do you even have a heart?" My heart sank and my voice cracked as I asked, "My—my sibling? Is dead?" As he heard my voice, father charged towards me.

Just then, a body shielded me; it felt as if all the dangers in the world were cast away, as if I were protected by everything that was harming me. It was my mom, shielding me from my father, but that heartless man had a smile on his face as he saw his lifeless wife's body drop to the ground.

A knife then approached me; my mom was no longer there to shield me. How am I supposed to protect myself? I had no idea what to do; I closed my eyes tightly and blocked myself from the knife using my hand.

As I opened my eyes, I saw my hand covered in blood as the knife pierced through my wrist. The warm drops of blood fell on my face, my eyes had turned blurry, and my consciousness was drifting away. 'Am I dying? Is this the end of my life? I don't have a meaning to live either... Mummy, I'm coming...'

Just then, I saw a boy wearing a cloak stabbing my father to death. And slowly everything became dark...

I woke up, gasping after hearing the bird's chirp. "Oh, another nightmare. I'm tired of them. Am I ever going to get rid of them?" I said in a tired tone while walking towards the kitchen to have my breakfast. I always thought about what happened to me 21 years ago. I was just 6 back then. I wonder what mistakes I made to end up like that.

As promised, I attended swordsmanship training to become a warrior. I ended up in a prestigious academy, with a fuzzy memory. I have quite a broken memory about my past.

At the academy, there were two people who were really strong; one of their names was Sepehr [Sky]. And the other one was Amir [prince]. They didn't seem to get along with each other. Everyone looked up to the two of them, accepting their strengths. But I preferred Amir, as Sepehr was a person who always compared me with other girls and hated my personality; we were quite the opposite. He knew about my family, which got on my nerves. He even knew the brutality of their deaths. His way of talking was always rude to me. My lost memory's answers were with him, but I never had the chance to ask him. He portrayed me as a criminal and used my scars and loneliness as evidence. What kind of sick game is it? On top of that, he broke the only memory I had of my mother, a necklace. Tell me something he didn't do to receive my hate. My relationships with my friends were not good either, and the reason could be Sepehr. He's been my study mate since my childhood.

But there's this incident that was the proof of my inability to make friends on my own: There was this time when I saw a girl who seemed kind of lonely; I saw myself in her, and I didn't want to lose the opportunity to help someone, at least this time. I made her my friend, and her name was Nora; we were on good terms. And just like that, our friendship and our friend group grew. I didn't want Nora to feel lonely in my absence. So, I asked her to make friends with Suri and Afareen [Queen], who were quite popular.

Nora and the other two girls, too, had gotten along just fine. Nora then told me that she had a crush on a boy; his name was Aydın; he was my horse-riding partner. We were both good friends, and I introduced him to her. Both became quite close together; I even wanted to plan their wedding. I succeeded, or so I thought... the two of them started hating me; basically, everyone did. Was it because I was no longer the friend of the popular kid? Or was it because I didn't know how to keep friends since it was my first time? Or was it because I look at the floor whenever a senior passes by? I respected them; I didn't look down on them. Or was it that I got jealous quickly? I'm immature! Please forgive me; I've made a lot of mistakes. My mistakes made me lose my mother; please forgive me. A lot of thoughts were running through my head at that moment, my eyes filled with tears and my mind with assumptions.

The reason why I lost them is something so...unexpected. I distanced myself from everyone after that incident... I suffered from a really serious abdominal injury because of a late-night attack at my cottage. I couldn't meet them for days, and when I did, they started ignoring me. I was afraid of getting ignored, as I was raised in such an environment. We even had fights pretty often. And eventually I lost all of them and continued living alone. I accepted my fate and stayed as it should have been.

Until I found him, Amir. Our friendship started after I told him something that he was still confused about. But he and I were friends to begin with. He had a prince-like aura around him; his blond hair looked like gold during the day, and his crystal blue eyes shone in the daylight. He had the warmest smile towards me and even offered me to stay at his house. Because of an embarrassing situation, I had burned my house down after I tried cooking something new.

We spent a lot of time with each other. For example, we planned on going to a restaurant as I wanted to be closer to him. He was the only person who acknowledged me. We usually had academy classes during the weekends, but we used to hang out with each other every day. Mornings I spent with Amir, and nights I trained myself to an extent to exceed everyone in class.

Days went by; we had gotten very close to each other. People even assumed we were a couple. And one day it turned out to be true. But there was something unusual about him. He always asked me questions about myself. I felt discomfort, but we've been together for two years, so I convinced myself, and I confessed everything to him one day.

After that, Amir always locked me inside a room and never let me out of it, except at the academy. It was cold, dark, and dirty in there. I got chills every time the wind passed my face. He told me that he did that to protect me, and I believed him. 'Naive little me, poor me.' Thoughts ran through my head.

It was a normal day; as usual, there was a huge fight at the academy. Sepehr and I turned the academy grounds into our battlefield. Our fight lasted long, and we even injured ourselves, just because he asked me about my dad. Amir had no intention of stopping us; he didn't seem too worried either; instead, he gave a creepy grin at us.

But one of our classmates ran to get our teacher to stop our fight. Just as our master rushed to the ground, he saw two of his students fighting and injuring each other. He jumped in and stopped the fight between us and gave us a lecture. We weren't punished, as we were in no condition to get one. We were given leave as our conditions were severe. Our master was surprised, as neither of us felt unconscious or gotten tired. He saw potential in us and used to tell us to work together, because if we did, we would turn out to be unstoppable. But of course, our enmity had not stopped there. We had turned our fights into verbal ones from then on.

Amir and I were on good terms, but ever since that fight with Sepehr, something had turned wrong within him. He had a disturbing type of aura around him; he even started ignoring me. I didn't like the way he acted or treated me. The room started feeling colder and colder. I acted as if I didn't notice; the supply of food had been cut down. The behaviour towards me also had changed, as if I were a slave bought from the black market. That's the treatment I received from an unusual him. I thought he was busy with his family or something else. Even Sepehr had not come to the academy for about a month, even though I couldn't care less about him. I was all alone; will this turn out to be good? I barely got any sleep at night. I wasn't doing well; my mental and physical health were both declining, and Amir then threw me out of his house. The dungeon I lived in was gone. I ended up with no food and no shelter.

Until a ray of mercy fell on me. I finally found someone I could rely on, or is my mind tricking me again? For now, I needed someone; someone to rely on.

She used to work at a cafe, and her name was Sadira [lotus tree]. I met her near a café where I rested my starving body. Her personality was like a sweet bay tree; she accepted me like accepting a puppy from the streets. The weight on my shoulder loosened up. She offered to take me into her house. I hesitated, but I was in need of a shelter. Once I have taken care of my needs, I promise to buy a house of my own.

Whenever I complained about myself, Sadira used to get mad at me, to help me realise the beauty within me, like this one day when I complained about my features in front of her: "When I first saw you, my head started writing a description about you, like: Your beautiful features marred by layers of mud and bruising. Aquamarine blue eyes, framed by long, dark black hair and set against pale white skin, would have been striking in any circumstance. But then, with your petite frame enveloped in filth and your delicate skin marked by injury, you were a strange juxtaposition of beauty and despair." She sounded like an expert at complimenting people. "When I saw you that day at the cafe, my saviour, you were like an angel come to earth. With hair the colour of a cortex and Hazel eyes that glowed like honey, your fair skin seemed to glow with an inner light. I could hardly believe that such a being had truly come to my aid." I described it to her in a dramatic tone of voice. She then hit my head with a spatula. "What was that for? And why do you have a spatula with you?" I asked with a confused tone. "To keep people like you in line, so they don't badmouth their own selves." She then continued to hit my head until I stopped. "Promise me you'll never leave me without telling me?" Her tone was serious, so I replied in a determined and promising tone, "I promise."

We both then went to bed. We turned out to be on good terms, even though I was worried about it since I thought I'd lose her too.

The thoughts had made me oversleep, and Sadira had to wake me up. The academy classes had gotten a lot tougher. But I nailed it, as it was quite easy for me, and of course, Sepehr, he too had come back after a long break. My late-night training at Sadira's house paid off.

After our classes, it was break time, and everyone was having their lunch. I had something to ask Amir: Why would he abandon me at a time like that? But it turns out he had found himself a new tool, a girl who turned out to be new at school; her name was Afareen; she worked as a chemist in the academy. She was the one who spread false rumours about me, even though I had just been joking with her a long time ago. She's the same Afareen who was my friend a long time back. I hated her to the core, but I didn't want to be the one who hated, so I controlled my hatred all the time.

Just as I was approaching Amir, she came out of nowhere and dragged me into the changing room, took a knife out of her pocket, and wrote large numbers on my neck. I held back as I could turn this into a big issue and kept quiet. She then said in an annoying tone, "This means that you won't die an easy death." Despite that, I tried warning her about Amir, "Wait, don't get along with him; he uses us. You'll get hurt!" She didn't bother looking at me and left me in the room, bleeding. I looked at my pathetic face in the mirror and realised that I was useless this whole time; "He was nothing but an extra to my life that seemed to have interrupted me. We weren't meant to be in the first place. How long am I going to suffer alone? I wish someone would at least understand me; I just hoped. I was a fool to consider his words on 'protecting me.'

A harsh reality,

> *'The petal has fallen from its flower. Why?*
>
> *Because of its loose bonds.'*

I came out of the room to find Sepehr and Amir fighting. I stopped the fight by coming between the two of them. Sepehr had a furious face while Amir had a bruised face with a grin, which showed that Sepehr had the upper hand. Sepehr, with a loud voice, spoke up, "If you ever hurt her or even look at her with your dirty eyes, I shall vanquish your very existence from this world and the next."

Wait a second, what is wrong with Sepehr? Why is he defending me? 'Doesn't he hate me?' Amir (seemed to had read my mind and asked), "You hate her as much as I do; now, why are you protecting her?" Sepehr then replied in a calm and polite way, "And why do you think that's real? And who do you think you are? I killed her father to protect her, so doesn't it mean I could even kill you if I want to?" I couldn't keep myself quiet after listening to what Sepehr told me: "I-it was you? ..." half of the words didn't even come out of my mouth through this shock.

"Yes, it was me. I had to hide the fact that I saved you so that I could protect you," said Sepehr in a soft tone.

"There we go, look at the new lovebirds." Interrupted Amir with an annoying tone. I went straight toward Amir and beat him up for the fact that he interrupted our talk, and his new tool injured me. Afareen too interrupted by coming out of nowhere and started fighting about the fact that I hit him. "It's uncouth to interrupt when two people are talking; I suppose the two of you mind that next time we meet." I've grown bold now; I can stand up for myself!

And just then, the teacher entered and called Sepehr and me to the director's office as we had gotten ourselves into trouble.

Confidential to the Main character

After Sepehr killed the female lead's father, he took her to the city to take care of her and tend to her. He got bullied by others for keeping a girl the same age as him in one house. Whenever he'd leave the house to get food, he'd come back injured. He used to get stoned by people, as he was misunderstood for a kidnapper, who kidnaps girls his age. But when he turned 18, he was filed to the king and was accused of kidnapping, but since she was old enough to take care of herself, he had abandoned her. Not completely abandoned since he's the one who paid the taxes, rents, and the requirements for her. He didn't stop supplying her needs, and on her birthday, he used to send her a letter saying that they were from her parents but were actually his own words. The fact that they are in the same school is that he wanted to protect her at all costs, and he's been with her since her childhood, protecting her.

Sadira was a lone girl living in her house. After her parents' divorce, she always yearned for a roommate but hated it when people got too touchy with her. Until she found the female lead in the corner of the cafe where she worked.

Chapter 2

Gladious

The director didn't intend to ask us the reason for the situation, as he knew that a bunch of 27-year-olds could handle their own selves. "I suppose the two of you already know the consequences of your childish behaviour." His voice was tough and echoed in the office. Sepehr and I did nothing but bow our heads down since we were aware of our behaviour. 'Sigh.' "You two are dismissed."

We weren't surprised that we were sent without our consequences given; instead scared of what was awaiting us in the near future.

While walking back, Sepehr interrupted my thoughts and asked in a soft tone, "If you don't mind, I would want to meet you somewhere outside of school." "Confusing, yet a creative way of asking someone out, you know?" I had a teasing voice while I replied to his request. His cheeks were flushed red. "You don't have to accept it if you don't want to..." Sweat ran down from the side of his head. Well, I want to find out about the way he killed my father. So, I agreed to his request and walked back home.

I saw Sadira waiting for me near the door. "What took you so long?" Her favourite spatula in her hand. "I got myself into trouble." A slump look on my face. "What did you do?" She asked in a motherly tone. "Let me freshen myself up so that I can spill the beans comfortably." She then let me inside her house and let me freshen myself up.

Later, I sat on the couch in the living room, sipped some tea, and let the cat out of the bag. And of course, I hid the fact about getting an injury. Since I didn't want to cause her any more trouble.

Her jaw dropped while she held the spatula in her hand. Thinking that I made a big mistake. "You must see the look on your face." The amusing situation made me giggle, like a baboon in a forest. "Wait a second, did this gloomy lady just giggle?" Her face lit with a smile as she noticed the little embarrassed look on my face. But can someone as caring as her ever be my friend? Her face then became serious; "So, you're telling me that the one who saved you and murdered your father is asking you out?" "That's quite the case now; well, to be honest, I have never spoken casually with him. Whatever I've done with him so far was fight with him." I looked into her eyes, asking for advice. "Don't worry, everything's going to be alright. Besides, he doesn't resemble much like the guy who took you in." She is more experienced as she had met many people in her life. That's the reason why I asked her; I'm somehow proud of my decision-making. I thanked her and went to bed.

Weird dreams, scary noises, and vulgar thoughts popped up in my head. Why is this even happening to me? Why do I see snow?

Out of nowhere? And a flower? I got goosebumps every time I saw that dream. And this was not the first time I'd seen it.

I woke up with a headache and had to go to the academy later. I saw Sepehr near the entrance gate waiting for me. What should I do in a situation like this? I just walked past him and felt rude. It was an awkward yet tiring day; I had to spar against Sepehr, as it was an assignment. He's tougher than I thought he would be. Never should've underestimated him.

Back at Sadira's house, I thought for an hour, planning our conversation at the place he told me to meet. Wasted my time and had to rush; I didn't quite eat anything and had to leave early, as the museum he told me to meet was pretty far from Sadira's house.

I reached there, and it seemed like he was waiting for me. I walked up to where he stood. And spoke to him respectfully, "Pardon my late arrival." "Don't be so formal towards me; accept me as your friend," he told me with a soft tone. After all you have done to me? Very well then, I shall use a better excuse for this. "Well, as you can see, I've never spoken to you like a normal person because, till now, whatever we've done was fight." I felt embarrassed as I told him this sentence, but it was reasonable. He then gave out a soft chuckle and said, "To be honest, all we've done so far was childish, isn't it right... eh..." He then paused for a moment and asked in a curious tone. "Wait, this might sound rude, but I never got to know your name." For some reason, I wasn't angry. But I had to act, "Are you joking?" 'Sigh.' "It wouldn't be noble of me if I didn't reply to a basic question. My name is Esmeray [Dark Moon]."

After I told my name, I looked into his eyes. And he too looked at mine with a soft gaze. A gaze that has a lot to say but says nothing. He stood tall, his lean frame standing out among the others in the surrounding, his silver hair, almost an anomaly, glimmered in the lamplight. But what really drew the eye was his piercing grey eyes, deep and intense, framed by strong eyelashes. His face could've been chiselled from marble, flawless and beautiful with sharp, angular features and a defined jaw. Though not overly muscular, his physique was still lean and toned, perfectly proportioned and elegant.

The silence was broken by him, as he asked, "Your eyes look like the ocean; I drowned in them and saw darkness; deep down was a small girl, who seemed to have given up but still hopes." His voice was calm and composed, but his words were loud. He sounded like the rain, but his words struck me like lightning. How can someone know so much just by looking in the eye?

I asked him questions about my past, how he killed my father, and why he killed him. But his reply was always, 'You'll know when the time comes.' I was noble enough not to get bothered by his simple answers. And asked him why he wanted to meet me. And he replied with an amused expression on his face, "Why do you noble ladies always think that when a guy gets close to a girl, it means that he likes her?" He had a point, but his eyes don't say the same thing as his mouth.

Hours passed, and it was almost time for me to go back, or else Sadira would kill me for being late: "Until we meet again." I told him with a smile and walked back home. The paintings in the museum were oddly familiar. Was it the flower? Or... the sword? I have no idea.

While walking back, my eyes started getting blurry, and my body turned pretty weak. Why does this feel painful while I take my steps back home? Scenes that were unknown to me flashed in my head; they seemed oddly familiar. A boy? A little girl on the bed? Unconscious? My head hurts as if it'll split in half.

After what felt like an eternity, I finally reached home. I saw Sadira doing the dishes at an hour when she usually works. I asked her in a weak tone. "S-Sadira, why are you back so early?" "I have been granted a day off, she replied. I had told you; have you forgotten?". "Oh, I see I must've forgotten." I suddenly lost my balance and fell on the wooden floor, making a loud thud sound. Sadira, without giving a second thought, turned the tap and rushed towards the entrance, where I was supporting myself from the wall.

She then supported me and helped me sit on the couch. Her face etched with concern, she started interrogating me like a mother to her child, "I see that you've started skipping your meals lately; why?" I had no words to answer that. But she continued, "Are you getting enough sleep?" No answer from my side, again. She then asked me nicely, "Why is it that you are not eating or sleeping?" I took a minute's silence and replied, "Well, I'm sorry for skipping my meals, but about my sleep schedule, I don't know what's happening to me. And also... I kind of got injured; it's an accident and not an accident at the same time." I then showed her my wound while talking. Her eyes widened, but she seemed confused as well, to see numbers as an injury. Her tone soft, "Don't worry; from now on, I'll take care of you, and you'll eat all your meals with me, okay?" She looked into my eyes with concern and tended to my wound. Her face had wrinkles while she did, but she was gentle so as not to hurt me. A smile then formed on my face. "I'm so glad that I have someone like you with me."

She then brought a bowl of soup for dinner. "From now on, leave the cooking to me, 'warrior of the future.' You must get all the nutrition you need to fight." That's what she called me. It felt cute yet awkward at the same time. But the warmth in her smile burned away all that day's pain. And it seems that I had gotten an infection and had to skip the academy that weekend.

And the next thing that happened to me was a proposal for the upcoming war. Sadira was really happy and gave me a tight hug. I was nervous, as I'll be participating in a real war; I had been waiting for this day my whole life. I was also informed that I had to attend the Academy not only on the weekends but every day.

Just as I reached there, I saw no one; the academy was empty. Am I the only one? Or am I early? Or am I late? Just then, I felt someone pat my shoulder. "Early as ever, Esmeray." It was Sepehr, his voice as soft as always.

During our strategy learning session, I asked our teacher, "Excuse me for interrupting the class professor, but why is it that only Sepehr and I have to participate in the war and why not the others?" Sir Miray fixed his glasses and asked, "Are you not comfortable with Sepehr?" I paused for a moment. "It's not that; it's just I'm curious about it, Sir Miray." I looked at the professor with curiosity. Sir Miray was the most intelligent strategic thinker in the whole of the Jabal kingdom. He knew our capabilities, so he had a smile on his face while he replied, "It's because of my approval on sending the two of you, as you are the only capable students I know. Also, it was the director's idea. Sepehr and I were surprised to hear what the teacher told us; we looked at each other with slightly surprised faces. So that's what the director was planning? These are the consequences of our actions? The class then continued after a small conversation. We were quite attentive to the class as we had to come up with tactics in the war if needed.

Hours passed; it was time to go back home. Suddenly, Sepehr approached me and asked if I could come to his house today. I was confused about the proposal, but I agreed and walked home with him; our teachers in the academy were surprised to see us together; I felt awkward; is it really the right choice? While walking with him, I asked, "Why is it that you want me to come over again?" "Practice; I want to spar with you," he told me with a smile on his face.

After walking for a while, we reached an isolated area; the building in front of me is his house. It's a mansion! He had two buildings, and the other one was yet to be built. He had both an annex and a main building. There was even a fountain just beyond the front gate. Guards were stationed all around the property. But still something felt missing, so I asked him, "Do you still feel lonely here?" His face darkened, but he smiled for me. "Yes, I do; well, you can assume that our childhoods can relate," he told me with a sad look on his face. "Oh, I'm sorry," I told him with a hint of guilt on my face. But he gave a reassuring pat on my shoulder and smiled.

We both talked for a bit at the dining table, making possible strategies together while having lunch. Well, he's a splendid cook.

Even though he had so many people working in his mansion, he was the one responsible for his own meals.

He then took me to his huge backyard. The leaves rustled, the cold wind playing with my hair, and made a beautiful sound. We then unsheathed our swords and started the duel. The two of us were equally strong. He was stronger and more dominant. His weapon was heavy. Meanwhile, my advantages were that I was strategic and quick. Moving like the wind, taking advantage of my light weight.

Our duel eventually ended; he then thanked me and was noble enough to ask me if he could accompany me in returning home. I declined since I enjoyed my time with me while walking.

Eventually, I reached home, and Sadira was pretty angry about my late arrival, so I told her where I had been this whole time.

"So, you went to this guy's house, studied with him, and also trained with him?" a cheeky smile on her face, "It's not like I did anything fishy; it's just that we are the only ones who are participating in this war, and he thought it would be a great idea." I told her nervously. She then finally granted me entry and asked me to freshen up quickly.

After obeying her, I noticed that something was wrong with her, so I asked, hesitantly, "S-Sadira, what's with that face? Are you angry?" I asked her nicely. "How could you not inform me of it? I was worried sick, you know? She seemed quite upset. "It was quite sudden, and I didn't know about it; please forgive me." She was pretty angry; she refused to cook dinner with me and even talk to me. But my stubbornness somehow made up with her.

Many days passed; at last, it was the last day of the academy. That day's training was unforgettable for both Sepehr and me. We took our swords and started sparring with each other. It was a tough duel as our will to fight and protect was the same. We didn't intend to give up at all. But we were eventually stopped by our professor. "That's enough for today, and don't exert yourself. Don't take it too lightly, as this is a real battlefield, and I don't want you two fighting each other, understood? The safety and, more importantly, the dignity of our kingdom are in the hands of the two of you. Don't mess up, and don't get too tense, alright?" The professor then warned us. We then kept his words in mind and walked back home.

After reaching, I saw Sadira rushing towards me. "I'm so happy, yet worried about you."Her warm hands wrapped my body, creating a perfect embrace. "Don't worry, I'll be fine, and I shall bring victory to us," I told her with full confidence. She said that she won't be here early in the morning and told me that she had prepared a farewell gift for me. "WOW! It's like a feast, Sadira." I looked into her eyes and told her. "Eat, my warrior; you need all the energy you can get." I then gave her a smile and started digging into the food. I then went straight to bed as she told me to.

The night passed. It was already time, and I was ready to go. Perfect, a situation like this? I've not bought a horse or formed a bond with it, and I have a war to fight today. I knew how to ride a horse, but never owned one. So I went to the stable nearby, where I looked around for the perfect horse. And at the corner was an isolated one. It was a beautiful black horse. I bought it as soon as I looked into its eyes, as if they're calling me. I hopped on it, and it didn't even flinch; normally, a horse would react if a new person sits on it, but it did not. So, I named him Kieran (dark one). It looked like we made a good team with each other and had created a bond. Guess I was in good hands today.

I then reached the designated place for the strategy meeting. There were many people from various kingdoms that were part of the empire. The meeting was not quite long, so we started our departure towards the battlefield earlier than expected.

While we were on our way, I felt awkward because I knew no one but Sepehr. He could see the awkwardness in me and got closer. He had a worried look on his face and asked, "You are the only lady here. Are you okay?" "It's not that; what I'm nervous about now is the war. We both should stick together, as we are the only ones from our academy, and we should keep our composure." I replied after observing the surroundings.

Minutes later, "I feel bored; let's have a conversation until we reach there, shall we?" he askedme with a comforting tone. "Sure, why not," I replied to his request. "First of all, what is the name of your beautiful horse?" he asked. "His name is Kieran. And what is the name of your horse?" I asked after looking at the pretty horse he was riding. "Her name is Eira (snow). I kept it, as she reminded me of the cool winter, and she had a familiar feeling in her." We continued talking with each other until a guy interrupted us. "Look, that is the student from the Jabal academy. Well, I wonder if your academy would survive because there's only one person coming." His tone made Sepehr really angry; just before he was about to answer, I directed him to rest assured and signalled him to leave it to me. "Oh, what a coincidence! I was wondering the same thing, if your academy would survive, as you didn't notice the other person talking to him. How I wonder what the faces you would've had if I had attacked you without you realising it! Picking a fight, huh?" I looked at them, determined, but they were ethical enough not to interrupt again. Sepehr then chuckled, "I can see why Amir is afraid of you." He told me in a teasing tone. I then changed the topic, not wanting to talk about him. "Anyways, I never thought that we'd ever go to a war together like this; everything we've ever done so far was fight with each other. In fact, I've never fought with anyone besides you. Will I be, okay?" I asked him in a curious tone, hoping for an answer. "If you've had a duel with me, then that means the rest of the world would be flies for you to deal with." Confidence was written on every part of him. "Pretty confident about your abilities, huh?"

Suddenly, a soldier came running towards the general. "We have bad news, sir!" he exclaimed with a breathless tone. "The enemy's forces are planning on attacking the nearest city." Just as the messenger passed the message, our general announced, "Everyone, it's a change of route; we'll be heading towards Nadia instead!"

After reaching the village, we evacuated the people to a safer place. And changed the strategy. We then got into our spots that we had planned for.

Just as we finished taking our places, the enemy forces entered and were welcomed with a surprise. Arrows were raining down on them. The strategy was good; the enemy had weakened, but they were large in number. We, on the other hand, were strategic and started coming out of the inns, caravans, and other places, as we were hiding, to ambush them at the right time.

Blood splattered on our armour and our faces. We could see that everyone was doing their best. But since it was everyone's first time in war, two people lost their lives. We couldn't do anything about it, but swore to avenge them.

We continued fighting and hoped that we would not lose more of our people. "Sepehr, why don't we try protecting the people who are injured instead of looking for the enemy? We're wasting a lot of time searching," I told him while fighting. "Good idea, now let's go!" We rushed over to the places where people were wounded and couldn't fight any further, as the enemy always attacks at the weak points. We took over most of the enemy's army, which let our general free the people who were kidnapped and enslaved.

It was a battle that continued for 8 days. We had set our camp inside a forest as there were many injured people.

It was our victory. We had won the battle! We were celebrating since it was our first war, and it turned out to be a victory! I then rushed towards Sepehr and hugged him tight. His hands wrapped around my slender figure. His grip was careful, as if he could break me if he held me any tighter.

He's warm; he smells like white oud. Strange, it seems very familiar...

Our general then ordered us to bring the evacuated people of Nadia. We stayed in our tents and lit up the campfire. We had to stay with our academy members as a group, but there were only two of us. It was embarrassing to stay with a guy, especially him!

I sat on a log while Sepehr lit up the campfire. He was wearing a coat. And his silver hair was still wet after the bath he took at the nearby spring. He was...just beautiful. Wait, what type of thoughts are running through my head? He too later sat beside me.

As the night got deeper, the weather got colder. A cold breeze had just passed by. I held my hands tightly and started rubbing them. Sepehr noticed and gave his coat to me. "Thank you, it wasn't necessary, really." A smile tugged on my face. He then got up from the log, got on his knee, stretched my hand, and kissed it. "I wouldn't be a man if I had not taken any action after seeing a lady suffer." His eyes looked into mine. Quite the charmer, isn't he?

He then sat beside me and kept his distance. And we started gazing at the stars, as the sky was clear that night.

Before I knew anything, it was morning, and Sepehr was nowhere near the tent. I thought of making myself useful and lit the fire for breakfast. Until I saw the man in the distance, one could not help but notice him returning from his hunt. His muscular frame was bathed in sweat, and his chiselled arms were covered with dirt and blood. He wore only a leather vest, revealing a powerful chest and biceps. But despite his rugged appearance, there was something striking about him. His hair, although flecked with some traces of grey, was still mostly pure white and shone brilliantly in the sunlight. Is it just me, or why is he looking like that?

"Good morning, Esmeray. I see you're up and are preparing something, huh?" He seemed too bright for the morning. "I thought of making myself useful, you know, just a little here and there." He then washed his hands and took over the cooking. "I've heard rumours about you burning your house down, wouldn't want a forest fire, lady." He teased while working.

We then quietly ate our breakfast and headed to the general's tent, as we had a meeting to attend. The meeting was about returning as there was news about simple attacks. And the general appointed a few to take care of the families of the ones who were martyred.

General, in my eyes, is really good-looking, I presume. He stands at an imposing height, his broad shoulders and muscular frame speaking of rigorous training and discipline. His brown hair is tied into a neat bun at the nape of his neck, and his eyes, a deep shade of amber, hold a watchful and intense gaze. A noticeable eyepatch covers his left eye, adding a touch of intrigue to his otherwise stern visage. Despite his intimidating bearing, there seems to be a sense of wisdom and determination in the set of his jaw and the lines that crease his forehead. I guess my imagination is going wild.

I couldn't concentrate on the strategy and had to ask Sepehr. Even though he is a 'no-nonsense' guy in these matters, he tends to make short stories long. Punishment.

After a few hours, we started packing up to return.

Confidential to the main character

While Esmeray was fighting for the kingdom, Sadira had also been working hard at the café for the two of them.

During that time, Sadira observed a regular customer with whom she had grown close. They both started hanging out with each other, and Sadira had company while Esmeray was gone. It made the café owner really angry, so she fired her from her job.

Our academy had regular classes; the fact that Sepehr and I had been to a war made the whole class envious. Which is why Amir started training even more. Not to be left behind.

The reason why Esmeray doesn't know what happened after the stargazing was because she had fallen asleep on Sepehr's shoulder, which brought a smile to his face. He then carried her inside the tent and laid her down. While he stayed outside, keeping a guard without interrupting her privacy.

Chapter 3

Lily

We finally reached the gates of the kingdom of Jabal, and they opened. I took a deep breath. 'That smells like home, all right.' Sepehr and I thought of meeting our master, so we headed towards our academy. As we reached there, we realized that everyone was attending class. We prepared ourselves to face them. We entered the class to surprise Sir Miray. As we entered, he rushed towards us and hugged us. "I'm proud of you two; I was given reports about your performance, and I'm really happy about them." Sir Miray smiled at us as he gave us the news. I turned my head towards the claps I heard given by our class. That's when I noticed a disgusting face. Amir, gritting his teeth, looked at the two of us. He did not seem happy, but rather envious…

I then looked at Sepehr and walked towards our seats in class, as we knew that we had nothing to do. We stayed there until it was time to go home. A few of the academy's seniors started insulting us, "How'd it feel to be the only girl there, or wait, even the only students of the academy?" "Probably they were assigned to take care of the horses instead." They laughed at us shamelessly. I couldn't shut my mouth, so I turned towards them and replied to their question in their own way, "Says you, who doesn't even know how to hold a sword. And at least we were chosen, unlike you, who were enjoying the peace we tried to maintain." Since then, they haven't even spared me a glance.. They thought that I was a blunt fool. I bid my farewell to Sepehr and took my leave.

I finally reached home and said, "I'm back home" in a familiar tone. Just as Sadira heard my voice, she rushed towards me and hugged me. "How I wondered you'd never come back," she told me while squishing me with a tight hug. "Shush, stop spouting nonsense! How could I ever lose in a battle in which Sepehr trained me?" "Oh, looks like someone believed in their friend's instincts quite a bit too much. Anyways, you must be tired; get some rest, and I'll go to work." She left for work while I was sleeping soundlessly.

I woke up and saw Sadira sleeping beside me. 'It makes me afraid that women like her were kidnapped because of their beauty.' I'm glad I was able to save their lives from being slaves.' I looked at her with a soft gaze until I realized the time and got ready for the academy. I changed and left home.

After reaching the academy, everyone was staring at Sepehr and me. But wait, why is the gaze falling on him by girls making me angry? What is this feeling? I entered my class, sat down at my desk, and gave some time for my thoughts to run wild. Until the teacher walked in, "Good morning class, there are a few announcements to be made. The first is the timing for our classes, which is going to change as the academy will now run during the weekdays for a couple of hours only. Combat training will happen alternately, and the days with no combat training will be taken for strategy training sessions. Also, I'm sure you all are aware of the banquet kept by the crown prince to honour the new war participants. Last but not least, I want all of you to assemble at the training ground now for combat training."

Just as the teacher had told, everyone had assembled at the training ground. The assignment for that day was to have a duel with either Sepehr or me. One of my classmates looked confident about getting the upper hand over me until I took my sword out and took my stance. Baris (My sword) had uneven edges, a lot of scratches, and marks. We started our fight; it didn't last long, as I had a better grip. And just like that, many more students fought us, but some of them had quit, while the others had lost. The only thing I could say is that Amir was the only one who gave me a tough time as my blade broke midst my duel with him. My expression darkened, and I threw the sword out of my hand; anger flared up within me, and great! I had to switch places with Sepehr. I had no other choice but to sit and watch Sepehr duel the rest of our classmates. But something was weird; as I looked at Sepehr, my anger subsided, as if looking at my mother walking up towards me after waking up from the dead. After I faced a 'life or death' situation with him, I feel different whenever I look at him. But why him? 'Is it because he gives off a familiar feeling? Or is it because he is the first one to make me feel like this? Thoughts ran wild inside my head; I couldn't even realize the time.

Sepehr then walked up towards me, handed me my leather bag of water, and said in a very gentle tone, "Good work today, Esmeray." I looked into his eyes and smiled at him, "Thank you; you did a great job yourself!" He then waved goodbye with a wink and disappeared into the distance. 'Wait, am I still sitting on the log that is in our training grounds?' I then quickly got up, grabbed my supplies, and took my leave towards home. I felt disappointed for what happened to my sword. 'That darn dull sword made out of a random ore; I should've bought a better one.' I grumbled as I walked back home.

After I reached home, I saw Sadira at the front door, and she said, "Looks like somebody had a bad day, huh?" "A bad day? The worst day! I was so disappointed in myself because my sword broke in the middle of my duel with Amir! I'm upset about it." I let out a 'humph' while telling her. She chuckled and walked towards me to comfort me by saying, "Don't be upset; anyway, we have a lot of time tomorrow. Why don't we go buy you a new sword? And I already have a friend who's an expert bladesmith." "You sure do know a lot of people, don't you?" I told her with a bit of a cheerful face.

Later, while talking, I thought of asking Sadira about her attending the ball, so I asked, "Hey Sadira, what are you planning on doing tonight? Since I won't be there at home most likely." "I probably am going somewhere to meet somebody; well, as you told, I have a lot of friends." She told me while she was doing some chores. "Where are you going? On a date with Sepehr?" She asked with one of her eyebrows raised and a smirk on her lips. My cheeks flushed red. "THAT IS NOT THE THING! It's just that I'm invited to the banquet held by the crown prince of the Jabal kingdom." Sadira's ears perked up. "A royal banquet? Meaning you have to dress up beautifully for it." Oh boy, I guess someone is (excited) to send me to the banquet well dressed. "Esmeray, get ready; we're going shopping!"

We were in the streets of Sakhar, the capital of Jabal. We were roaming from shop to shop, looking for the best dress. And ended up buying a lot of accessories to go with the dress. Too much for a single evening.

It was finally time, and I was dressed up by Sadira. She said that she wouldn't leave until she saw me 'dressed up.' And here I am at the palace, stuffed inside a gown.

As I walked through the palace , I reached the palace's banquet hall. Really pretty, to be honest. But why doesn't it astonish me? As if I've known better? And as I walked, I saw Sepehr wearing white as usual, but formal clothes had a different feeling; I was mesmerised. A dignified and distinguished figure. He wore a crisp three-piece white suit, the only touch of colour being the jet-black accessories that adorned him. His hair, a silvery grey, was neatly combed, and his once-grey eyes now seemed to reflect the bright light of the hall, almost seeming to gleam golden. His eyes immediately reached mine. They were soft as always and warm like they had reflected. I stood there, frozen, only looking at him, admiring his beauty.

I gathered some courage and walked towards him. "Well reserved, Sir Berfin," I told him while chuckling in embarrassment. "Very demure, Lady Esmeray. I didn't expect you to call me out by my surname. And as you can see, this place is filled with nobles. I advise you not to." he told me with a teasing tone. And just before I could give him a reply, an announcement was made: "Ladies and gentlemen, we had our young warriors fight their first war this month. They've all assembled here, as per the crown prince's invitation. This banquet is held to honour them and thank them for their sacrifices. To celebrate it, let's have a calming dance, shall we?"

Sepehr's eyes darted towards me. The fact that I knew what was coming next brought goosebumps. "Sepehr, I don't like dancing" "Lady Esmeray, I would love to have you as my dance partner; it would be great if you'd accept my invitation." He interrupted before I could finish my sentence. But my heart didn't agree with my condition, and I ended up dancing with him.

He had a look on his face, astonishment. The kind of reaction I would expect from anyone I would dance with. He asked in a soft and calm tone, "Esmeray, you are able to dance, adding to that, with perfection and no flaws. How is it possible?" "Well, my mom used to teach me when I was a child; she seemed to dislike it but never really gave up on it" I told him while dancing. He didn't seem as surprised, but it seemed rather strange, as if his suspicion about something was getting clearer.

As we kept dancing, a warm blush spread across my cheeks. What is wrong with me? I also saw Amir standing with the crowd, his teeth gritting. He knew the fact that I hated dancing and had rejected many proposals from him. He seemed quite mad about me choosing Sepehr as a 'dance partner.'.

I started feeling guilty and a bit uncomfortable. And to freshen up my mood, Sepehr took me to the garden, and after a while of taking fresh deep breaths, he requested in a pleading manner, "Would you stay at my house, just for tonight, please?" "Fine, I suppose." 'Seriously, Esmeray? Are you kidding me?' I smacked my head really hard in my imagination. Who would accept a request to stay the night at someone's house? And on top of that, it's a request pleaded by a 'male.' 'Well, it was pretty late, though.' I tried convincing myself as I walked with Sepehr to his house. 'Late? Are you sure that's a good explanation for you to give Sadira if he *censored* you?' Whoa, looks like my thoughts are running wild. Let's not ruin the mood, shall we?' I then shut those voices off and followed Sepehr.

We reached his house, and he said, "Just follow me; I've got a surprise for you." We then reached his rooftop. "It seems someone likes stargazing? That's why I remodelled and decorated this place for you," he told me with a soft gaze. "It's beautiful, Sepehr." He took a breather as he didn't know that he was holding it. I walked towards the edge and sat on the wall; Sepehr too came and sat beside me. We then gazed at the stars for quite a long time. Until I interrupted the silence with a question, "How'd you know I liked stargazing?" "I don't know, maybe during the war, when you were looking at the stars with joyful eyes and slept on my shoulder," he told me in a teasing tone. "I slept on your shoulder?" My face couldn't hide the blush. Sepehr chuckled as he looked at me, flustered by my own actions.

We gazed at the stars for a long time. We saw a shooting star pass by. The sky was clear, and it was filled with beautiful stars, and the moon had a beautiful crescent shape. Sepehr, after looking at the shooting star, said, "Don't you think the moon belongs to the sky?" He told me while his cheeks flushed red. I thought for a moment, giving my fish brain some time to understand. 'Wait a second, 'Sepehr' means the sky and 'Esmeray' means the moon. Does that mean he's proposing to me, saying that I belong to him?' My cheeks flushed red; the word 'no' never seemed to have existed in the dictionary for me if it was for Sepehr.

And after some time, while another shooting star passed, I answered, "Yes, I do think the moon belongs to the sky." He then looked at me with eyes filled with life. The grey in his eyes had more stars than there were in the sky that night. He then held a strand of my hair and said in a gentle tone, "I love your long hair, never ever cut it, please Esmeray!" A smile played on my lips. I'm glad that someone liked my long hair. Which I had put lots of effort into growing because of the lack of nutrients. "I won't!" And that night, a gesture was done with me for the first time, something no one had ever done to me. A kiss. His lips and my lips were pressed against each other tightly. My eyes widened when he did that; that's when another shooting star passed, making me realise,

> *'The fallen petal has got its life back because of the rain.'*

After something like that happened, he took me inside his house; he then asked, "Do you want to eat something?" Asking for food after you did something like that? That's exactly why I accepted your proposal; I'm proud of my decision. I hid my stupid pride within and replied, "I wouldn't mind eating, but if you insist." He then entered the kitchen and tied the apron around him. And then started cooking something. Wait a second, that apron reminds me of the books Sadira reads about. Why the hell does he seem so handsome in something women should wear? What about a maid's dress? Why? Am I going crazy like Sadira? She and her obsession over fictional men. 'Mental nosebleed.'. I matured myself and asked, "Would you mind me helping you?" "Of course not; it's okay if you want to." He replied gently. I smiled and entered the kitchen. I took over the task as an expert at cutting the vegetables and meat. He said with a smirk formed on his lips, "Looks like someone is good at handling a knife." I should've controlled my bluntness: "If a sword, why not a knife?" The two of us then finished cooking. And set the table up together. He then darkened the room as we were going to sleep after eating and lit just a few candles around the table. He then pulled the chair for me and sat on the other side of the table. We started eating after both of us were comfortable. "Sepehr, why did you propose to me?" My blunt question made the mature me choke on my food. 'Are you out of your mind!' Exclaimed the mature side of me. 'Forgive me, but I couldn't hold it in.' I then looked at Sepehr, and he didn't seem so flabbergasted by my blunt question and replied in a calm voice after wiping his mouth, "It is a feeling I have felt for you since quite a long time, and I waited for the right time to propose." 'He prepared so much for me.' The romantic me was moved and started tearing up inside of me.

I then forced myself to shut my mouth to avoid a blunt question. "Sepehr, the food tastes delectable." Sepehr then smiled at me and replied, "I'm glad you liked it." I smiled back at him, "I thought you'd compliment the taste of the food after I'd done washing the dishes…" His mischievous smile made me want to punch his face. But how could I possibly hit such a handsome face? "Are you going to sleep with your unmentionables?" Okay, yeah, I take back what I just said; I'm going to punch him. "Well, it was your plan to bring me to your house, so I thought maybe you'd be ready for a situation like this." I was noble enough to hide my true intentions and replied maturely. "Well, I suppose I can hand you my robe or a spare shirt." He replied and got up from the table.

The dinner was officially over, and now it was time to go to bed. "Sepehr, it'd be a burden if you did much on your own. So, allow me to do the dishes while you prepare a room for me." Sepehr gave an understanding nod and let me take over the prep sink. I later washed the dishes while he cleaned the guest room for me; he also gave me a change of clothes to wear, just like he had promised. I bowed a small 'good night' and walked into the room. I changed my clothes and plopped onto the bed. My eyelids started getting heavy, and eventually, I fell asleep.

A ray of light fell into my eyes and woke me up. I heard noise coming from outside. I then freshened myself up. I then opened the door and saw him cooking breakfast for both of us. Right after I saw his shiny, morning-like hair, I greeted him gently, "Good morning." He saw me, and the first thing he did was tease, "Good morning; I thought you'd keep sleeping the whole day like a cat." 'Meow' the sound echoed in my ears. "Yeah, yeah." I intentionally said the word twice.

He then gestured me towards the table and pulled the chair for me. We started eating breakfast after he too had settled down. While eating, I just realised that I had to wear something for the academy. "Sepehr, about classes—" before I could finish my sentence, "It's the weekend; we have no classes today." His gentle and stern tone let out a sigh of relief after understanding the situation. But why's he cooking when he has maids of his own? I then finished my food and looked at Sepehr. He let out a long sigh and replied, "Cooking is my hobby, and a death by poison is the most disgraceful death." Did he just read my mind?

After we finished our breakfast, he took me to a room. "This is the reason I called you to my house." He said as he led me towards his armoury. "I've brought you here so that you can choose your sword. Wait, I actually want the weapon to choose you." His words didn't make sense, but they sounded wise.

He wrapped a cloth around my eyes and turned me around. "Walk towards the side that is calling you." His words translated into instructions in my head and turned into directions that felt right. I then walked in a direction that felt as if it pulled me towards it by tying tight knots. And as I opened my blindfold, I saw an obsidian sword, it's not entirely made up of Obsidian since it would make the sword brittle. But the edges seemed sharp enough to cut anything in its way. "Looks like the sharpest one chose you as its master; now accept it as my gift." He said, looking into my eyes. "Why are you giving this to me?" I asked him with a concerned look. He smiled gently towards me and said, "Since you broke the other one, this one is a replacement." I smiled gently, and I ran towards him and hugged him as tight as I could. I mumbled on his shoulder, "Thank you; I don't know how to repay you." He hugged me back and said, "There's no need to repay me. And besides, this is one of the many gifts I'm going to give you, as you are mine. Lady Esmeray belongs to me, and me only." He got on his knee and kissed my hand. And looked into my eyes with a promising gaze. "My lady, would you allow me to take you to a dinner date tonight? Also, let's make it a double date, shall we?" He winked at me, with his long, delicate, grey lashes bouncing, after convincing me to attend it, no matter what.

I reached back home with the same clothes I wore to the ball. I swiftly made it to my room and changed into comfortable ones. Just as I exited my room, I saw Sadira sitting on the couch, looking blue. I then walked up to her and asked, with the softest voice, "What happened? You don't look so good." I waited for a while patiently for her to answer until her hoarse voice from all the crying was heard: "I—I lost my job." And right after I heard what she told, my body moved on its own and embraced her from behind. She seemed to have cheered up a bit. And to help her out more, I gently started caressing her hair and said in a soft tone, "I know that you loved your job so much, but don't worry; I'm sure the reason you lost it must've been because something better is waiting ahead for you. Maybe the job offers you're going to get next is something you dreamed of in your childhood. And perhaps if you go out with me this evening, it might cheer you up a bit, right?"

The clock ticked, and Sadira picked up a dress for me to wear. 'Why is she so good at selecting clothes?' A turtleneck neckline, without sleeves and with a bodice so beautifully embroidered. The waistline perfectly fitting my waist and a beautiful long silhouette, with the hemline almost touching my toes. I wore black gloves to enhance the outfit. And, yes, Sadira did my hair, as she loves doing so.

Sadira with a simple dress looked like a flower blossom. Her hair was going so well with the navy-blue dress. And the gold accessories made her look so beautiful. She looks so pretty, yet that puts them in danger, like the war that happened a few days ago. I hope that everything goes well.

We then finally reached the place I was asked to meet at that time. As we walked, we saw Sepehr holding a bouquet of flowers. He handed the bouquet to Sadira and said, "Ms. Amani, allow me to introduce myself, I'm Sepehr Berfin and you can call me Sepehr. I asked your dear friend out, and she accepted it. Please give me your blessings for keeping her happy." After listening to what he said, she seemed really happy and wrapped around me really tightly. "You could've told me, you know? Who cares now? It's a wonderful surprise!" I returned the hug. "Sadira, I apologise for smiling while you were in so much sorrow." I looked into her eyes with guilt and concern. Sadira then held both of my hands tight and said, "Nonsense, when you're happy, I'm happy with you as well." A soft smile spread across her face. And right after that interaction, Sepehr had a smirk on his face and whispered something in Sadira's ear. Her eyes widened after listening to what he said. She looked at him in confusion and asked, "H-How do you know him?" 'Who is 'him'?' I wondered, but I patiently waited, as I was really interested in the conversation the two were having.

After that interaction they had with each other, a man came walking towards us. The man stood tall and straight, his figure lean and imposing. His dark brown hair, the colour of polished wood, was neatly parted and fell just above his broad shoulders. His eyes, a rich cocoa colour, held a gentle warmth, and his face, although stern, was not without a hint of kindness. Despite his imposing height and stiff bearing, his gestures were soft and unhurried, giving him an air of quiet confidence and refinement.

"Lady Amani, long time." He had a soft voice as he spoke to Sadira, calling her by her surname. "It really has been quite a while, Sir Demir." She had a soft smile on her face as she replied to him. The two of them seemed quite close. She then looked at me with a soft smile and said, "Now that Mr. Sepehr has told me something about the two of you. I guess I should stop hiding and tell you about us." She smiled and looked towards the man and nodded towards him. He then smiled at her and turned towards Sepehr and me. "Lady Esmeray, as this has been kept from you, I'd like to disclose it. I apologize. Lady Amani and I are betrothed." 'Betrothed' means they are yet to be married? I felt really happy for them, but I pushed the floor under my shoe and ran towards Sadira and gave her a hug.

The four of us then walked inside and enjoyed our time conversing with each other. As the evening grew dark, I returned home 'penniless.' But convincing Sepehr, was hard. We had a fight on 'who's going to take care of the small gathering financially.' Since Sepehr was the one who suggested it, I thought of bearing the expenses and ended up returning penniless.

A week had passed with nothing going wrong. We were in the middle of our exams Luckily, I aced everything. And Sadira was really proud about it.

Except there was something bothering me. It was the absence of Amir and Afareen from our academy. I was so lost in thought that day that the only thing that found me was Sepehr's intense gaze towards me. "May I have your attention!" Sir Miray was really respectful towards his students as he said that. Our attention darted towards him. "As we're done with many classes and tests.

We are glad to tell you that this batch has successfully passed and is going to graduate. Unfortunately, two of our students wouldn't be attending it, as they are out of town." I'm glad we're graduating. But the sudden disappearance is bothering me.

I was bothered the whole day that I didn't eat anything at all. At the end of the day, while we were leaving, I walked towards Sepehr. "Sepehr, wait, I have to ask you something." I asked him in a pleading voice, "What is it?" he asked while calming me down. "Will you help me look for Afareen today?" I asked. "Wait, why do you want to look for her, I don't like her, since you two dispute each other!" He looked into my eyes, with anger flared up in him. "Quit whining, and help me. It's been bothering me for quite a long while. Can you? Please?" I had a puppy face when I asked him. "Ok, fine, let's go." He wasn't willing, but he had to as 'it's me.'

The thought that I had still hid the fact about my wound from him crossed my mind. What would happen if I told him?

We took our leave on horseback and started looking for her. We looked for her everywhere and found nothing. We then lost hope and started riding back home. The search got me so fixated on it that I couldn't eat or drink anything. Until I felt something weird in the ally, we just passed by. "I sense something there." I told him, and he started walking there with me.

A woman covered in blood and flies flying around her. "What is thi—-" a loud thud.

Confidential to Esmeray

The man whom Sadira used to meet was Başar Demir. She didn't want her friend to know and waited till the right time. The reason they got engaged was that they had known each other for more than a year and had fallen for each other.

Başar had accepted Sadira as her assistant. Meaning she is a nurse. Something she dreamt of. Basar was a well-known physician and was an expert in his field.

Extra

This is how Sepehr felt when he saw Esmeray at the banquet: As she walked into the room, her presence immediately commanded attention. Her dark black hair, like the night, fell in long, silky waves to her waist. But it was her eyes that truly mesmerised, a deep and soulful blue that held an almost otherworldly beauty. She wore a classic black formal gown, the tight-fitting fabric accentuating her slender figure. A pair of matching gloves covered her hands, and a glittering diamond necklace graced her neck. Is she who she is, or am I looking at someone inhuman? The moon is looking envious towards her. Her beauty is unparalleled.

Chapter 4

Oleander

My eyes then opened to see Sepehr, right in front of my eyes. "Wh-Where am I?" It turns out I'm on Sepehr's lap. I then immediately got up. "What happened?" He had a gentle yet concerned smile on his face, "You fell unconscious right after you saw Afareen's dead body. "She's dead?" Stands up immediately. My body couldn't take the immediate action and I started to stumble. Sepehr then quickly held me and carried me in a bridal carry. "I'm taking you home. Your body is too weak. I'll come and discuss with you about the incident later." His grip was firm on me, and his gaze soft. He then mounted me on my horse and sat behind me. "What about—" He then looked towards Eira and walked Kieran towards her. "Eira, go back to the mansion. And when I'm back, I'll make sure to give you sugar cubes." Eira then galloped back on her own. Sepehr rode Kieran back to Sadira's house. My body leaned on Sepehr's body. It feels like the warmest thing I've ever felt. "Can this moment be forever?" What did I just say? "I promise to keep you like this, once you're completely recovered," Sepehr replied in the softest tone, while he was completely focused on the path ahead of him.

The next day, while I was resting in my room. "Esmeray I'll be leaving for work, I'll be back by evening. You've exerted yourself a lot these few days, so take plenty of rest." Sadira's voice reached my ear from the living room. I then got up from the bed and rushed towards the living room. "You found a job already?" She then smiled at me and said, "Mr. Demir has accepted me as his assistant and has promised me that he'd teach me a lot of things during that time." I was glad to hear that. I then hugged her tightly, but my body isn't helping me much at the moment. "Esmeray, I guess you've given your body too much stress. The number of things you're thinking is unhealthy. So, keep yourself calm." She reassured me and helped me walk back to my room. "Esmeray, I guess I'll stay. Your condition isn't looking good." She looked into my eyes in concern.

"No! It's alright, I don't want you to skip work just because of me." I pleaded her until she got convinced and took her leave, for work.

A knock was heard on the door. Visitors at this time of the day? But Sadira isn't here. Why are they here? The knock got louder. I then got up from the bed and walked towards the door. The door opened, and there stood, "Sepehr? What are you doing here? What about academy—" he then pressed his index finger on my lips. "Shhhh, stop talking, and no one is home, right? My eyes widened, and I nodded to the question about being alone at home. He scooped me up in his hand, closed the door and carried me to my bedroom. "Sepehr, what is it that you are here for?" He then gently laid me down on my bed. A smile on his face, "I came here to check on you. I was quite surprised by what happened yesterday. So, I wanted to check up on you." I smiled gently at him, "I'm alright now, you don't have to worry about me." Sepehr's eyes then turned serious, "Since I'm here, I might as well give you the report about Afareen's case." I then stiffened myself up. "Go ahead, Sepehr." He then had a stern look on his face as he spoke, "She died not long before we found her body. But it was confirmed that her death was a murder." My eyes widened in shock, 'Was she an enemy of someone who would keep a strong enmity towards her, to kill her?' I then looked at Sepehr and asked, "How brutal was it?" Sepehr was a bit surprised, but he knew what my next question would be and continued, "There were bruises on her neck, that showed that she was choked. And she had a wound on her chest that seemed to have been the result of her death." After listening to what Sepehr said my body had gone cold. I phased out, my thoughts were going to kill me one day. It felt like I was standing in the middle of a storm, with light clothes on.

Until I felt the warmth of the sun reaching my body. It was so warm that I would gladly burn away for it. Sepehr's hands were wrapped around me tightly, which created the perfect embrace. "It's hard to take in a lot within yourself, but it's alright Esmeray. Everything will be alright." His warmth comforted me as if it were some sort of spell. He then broke the hug and looked into my eyes. "I wish to take away whatever you've gone through and listen to whatever you're thinking." His lips were then pressed against mine. Making me realise the amount of love Sepehr has for me.

Sepehr left. And hours later that Sadira came back home. We had a warm dinner together. And while helping her wash the dishes, I spoke to her in a gentle tone, "Sadira, well, I wanted to tell you that I'm going to graduate at my academy tomorrow. And I think after this, I might have to stay in the battlefield for a long time." Sadira was glad that I was going to graduate but there was a hint of sadness in her eyes. "I'm going to be alright, don't worry." She gave me a tight hug and said, "I'd love to boast about calling my roommate a war hero. But be careful, okay?" A tight embrace was given by her from behind. "I'll miss these hugs." Sadira's grip tightened. "Stop talking, as if you're going to die early." My eyes began to fill up with tears. But I controlled them in.

It was morning; I had a dream about facing myself and another young girl who stood beside my reflection. What is wrong with these dreams? They really are giving me a headache…I got up to see that Sadira had already left; her work is more strenuous and harder than she thought it would be.

I was finally graduating after years of constant training and hardships. I learnt and found quite a few things along the journey of sword training.

I reached home after a long day of celebrating. And while I was preparing to get some rest. A letter arrived from the imperial palace.

It was an order from the king to participate in the war, which included a conquest to conquer the rebellious kingdom near Jabal.

I then ran towards where Kieran was kept and mounted him immediately. I then started to ride towards Sepehr's house.

I don't know why, but I can't stop thinking about Sepehr, why? My body is moving on its own, I don't know what to do after reaching there, my body isn't listening to me, and Kieran is also acting weird. "Kieran, I don't want to go anywhere. And I know that you know that I'm a bit disturbed." Kieran just kept galloping forward, as if he knew that going there was the best option.

I then let Kieran do what he thinks is best. Until Kieran rushed into Sepehr's gate and started rearing up. He was uncontrollable at that moment. "Easy boy, Easy..." I tried calming him down with a soft tone. But he didn't seem to listen to me.

And after listening to the commotion outside, Sepehr rushed in and calmed Kieran down. He also helped me get down on my two feet. "Thank you, Sepehr..." I breathed a long sigh, not knowing I was holding my breath.

He then guided me inside his study... He seemed to have a lot of paperwork, already. "Ah, Esmeray, did you receive the letter from the king? Shall we skip the part about Afareen's body going missing?" I then turned my attention back towards Sepehr, "I indeed did, and it seems to be a conquest of a rebellious kingdom." I avoided asking him the thing I came here for, in a hurry. He then smiled softly and said, "It indeed is, but there is a twist, the emperor is a man of surprises, he said that, the warrior who takes down the throne holder of that kingdom, owns it..." The condition given is really uncanny... "I'm sure many warriors are flamed up to be 'that warrior'. What about you Sepehr?" He thought for a while, but shortly replied, "I don't know, I guess I'll just keep a low profile, and do what I can do." Well, the answer does sound like Sepehr, alright. Later I realised, that coming here was a better idea after all.

Weeks passed, Sepehr and I spent our time training together. And occasionally went out for walks, where we spoke with many children. And played with them.

A day before the departure, I was with Sepehr. At his house, we sat near the fireplace, covering ourselves with the same blanket. The recent troubles forgotten. The sky outside was grey like Sepehr's eyes. And the occasional sound of the rain, synced with the sound of the wood shifting in the fireplace. It wasn't raining heavily, but small water droplets did fall… I then reminded myself of the day we spent with the children, playing "Sepehr, how many children do you want, after we get married?" His cheeks flushed red, was it because of the heat or my question? He looked at me in a soft gaze and replied, "I really don't mind how many. It depends on you." I smiled at his reply and said, "I want 6 children! 3 girls and 3 boys." Sepehr's eyebrows raised after listening to the number. It's not something so easy to make, but the cheerful expression and the blunt claim brought him laughter. And after a small conversation, our lips pressed against each other tightly. Until we lost our breath.

The day of departure, at Sadira's house. I saw her doing some paperwork at the study. I kept a glass of water on her table and asked "How was your day at work?" she replied with a smile on her face, "It was tiring but I'm able to learn so many things, but I'm glad I can do what I once dreamt of when I was a child." I gave her a tight embrace. "I'm glad you're enjoying your work, but I hope that you don't exert yourself to the point of passing out, please." Sadira smiled, but I knew that she wouldn't listen to me. I then broke the embrace and said, "I'll be taking my leave then, I won't be here for a while." Sadira stood up from the chair and held my hand tightly, "Please come back, without hurting yourself, please." Her eyes pleaded. I smiled at her and took my leave.

I went to my mother's grave, kept some flowers, and asked her for her blessings. I then looked at the grave beside my unborn sibling's, it was my father's. I clenched the soil on it and started tearing. "It's been a while, father. I missed you, and I have never forgotten to love you." Just then, a reassuring hand patted my shoulder. "I wish to be the most important man in your life after your father, Ez." I turned my head towards the voice and saw a man who shined as bright as the sun behind him. "Sepehr, you already are the most important person in my life."

We then went to the spot where they had called us for the assembly. We then set off with the rest of the troop. But this time, the level of insecurity was higher, as Sepehr and I were the youngest. A deep and mighty voice announced, "Everyone! Our destination is the Karanlık kingdom. Keep your eyes peeled after reaching there, as the people there are known to be sketchy!" People of Karanlik are known as 'the followers of their name.' As the name of the kingdom suggests, 'darkness'. Those people are known to deceive and break contracts.

As we rode closer towards the kingdom, cold wind started blowing. The forest had an eerie feeling. There were no leaves on the trees, and the clouds seemed to deny the entrance of the sun.

And just then, an arrow came and shot one of the warriors. "Everyone, as expected, these backstabbing people have attacked us without following the contract!" Our general alerted us, and we dismounted our horses and got into our positions for the battle.

"S-Sepehr are you sure we're standing in the right place?" I asked Sepehr while my breath was restless. His gentle hand patted my shoulder, "I am a hundred percent sure."

"But Sepehr, we're on the front line!" Sepehr looked determined and unsheathed his sword. I then took a deep breath and unsheathed my sword as well.

The battle began, and people's lives were on the line in this conquest. And the person withholds the power of 'a war hero' and owns the kingdom if he takes the throne holder down…

The conquest goes on; it's almost been a week since we've entered the battlefield. We've built our base in the places which has been conquered.

At the base, we discussed the plan on raiding the palace, as we had gotten closer to the capital. General suggested a strategy, but I found flaws in it and looked at Sepehr, he then understood my signal, and said "General, I suppose the plan has flaws." And started suggesting to him strategies that might work.

After a long meeting, we finally got time to rest. "Sepehr, the look in your eyes suggests that you'll pass out from exhaustion. So, I'll be the one keeping watch." Sepehr's eyes widened, and he replied immediately, "I'm not going to leave a woman alone outside, and worse, during a conquest while protecting me, I can't let that happen!" His body was too weak to handle the pressure, Stagger. "Easy there, you can't even stand on your legs right now." I then supported him towards our tent. "Sepehr, take some rest, later you can be the one guarding, but tonight I want you to rest, for your fatigue is too much." He had no choice but to listen to me. He then entered the tent and fell asleep.

I was sitting outside the tent, looking out for any danger. But instead, I found two friends talking with each other. "Hey, did you see that woman in the battlefield?" He asked. "Of course I did. There is no man in our troupe who hasn't. She is stunning for a woman who wields a sword!" He exclaimed in awe. The two men stood near the tree and continued their conversation. "She indeed is; I wish my wife could look that beautiful." "I can totally relate to you, man! But have you observed her eyes?" His question seemed to have caught the man's attention. "I did, they are an eerie blue, such blue only exists in royalty or the nobles." "What if she is a witch?" That question made my heart skip a beat. "If she is a witch, then she will be burned to death. And we don't want to lose such a beauty. Why not keep our suspicions to ourselves?" Their denseness had saved my life. But in an era where women are burned for the misunderstanding of being a witch, it is tough to live an educated woman's life. I sighed to myself and looked at the sky. Looking at the sky always calms me down. I then chuckled to myself, 'Is that why the love of my life's name means 'the sky'? I was then lost in my thoughts.

Hours passed, and the night became darker. The only source of light was the moon. The surroundings were silent. Strange, it isn't supposed to be this silent. While my mind was somewhere else, I felt a sudden dizzying and lost consciousness.

Gasp! Water was splashed on my face. The surroundings were dark and cold. My legs, my hands and even my neck were bound with chains. A piece of metal was tied around my mouth, which prevented me from speaking. "Welcome, Esmeray!" A familiar voice was heard. Something I didn't want to hear. "It's been a long time since we've met." He seems to be getting on my nerves right now. "You! Take her mouthpiece off, now!" He ordered the woman standing behind me. "Amir! What are you doing? I thought you already gave up about 'that'!" His sinister laugh was giving me the urge to punch him. Clink! The chains straightened up when I moved closer to him. "What is that you want—" blood dripped from my nose. "Huh?" My eyes got blurry and my body was burning. "Wh-what did you put on the mouthpiece?" He smiled at me and spoke in an annoying tone, "It is a factor that will make you regret your decision." What? He then gestured the woman, "Do as we planned!" The woman hesitated, but approached me and chugged down a whole bottle of liquid inside my mouth. It tasted sweet. But suddenly everything started getting blurry in front of me. It felt as if my insides were on fire. My blurry sight had turned red, and my eyes started tearing blood. I had a runny nose, although it was blood that came out instead. Cough cough! Blood. Was there any part of me that didn't bleed? "Why are you doing this to me?" I could no longer see his face. "Do it!" The woman then suddenly caught hold of my hair and slash! Cuts them. "M-my Hair! My Hair! How dare you? You knew that I held them dear to me, so why? Why did you cut them?" Anger, frustration and tears filled me. Clink clink the chains straightened and the pull had caused wounds on the places where the chains were locked.

"You really are a stubborn woman, aren't you? The amount of poison you took in could've already killed an ordinary person."

He then signalled the woman to do something, again. The woman hesitantly brought a knife and dipped it in some liquid. Slash! Makes a cut on my skin. "Wait! Remove the armour she's wearing and make cuts on every part of her body, except her face, got it?" The woman flinches at his orders and starts unbuckling my armour. I then saw Amir turning his face away from me. Avoiding my armour-less state. The woman grabbed the knife and started obeying his orders. Slash! Slash! "I-I'm not an object; I'm a lady just like you…" she flinched and trembled in fear and guilt. But I guess the wounds inflicted on me by her are because she's getting threatened or blackmailed; I know she has her reasons.

The poison on the knife had caused the wounds to bleed more than they should and had caused a pool of blood. My eyes started getting blurry and I couldn't see anything. It felt as if every part of my body was being pierced with millions of needles. "Are you done? It would be disrespectful for me to see a woman without her armour, which would make her chest look more prompt, and I wouldn't dare touch a woman until we're wed, it's disrespectful for her." He made claims that would sound good if I was not tortured. He then said this in a tone full of concern "Please don't do this, don't do this to my broth—"

Just then, a loud noise was heard, 'Did someone break something?' And then a familiar voice was heard, 'Esmeray!…' The sound started to fade and my vision began blurry and suddenly everything became dark.

Confidential to Esmeray

Just after Sepehr heard the loud thud from outside, he rushed and saw that Esmeray was gone. He then armed himself and started searching for her. He searched for her everywhere in the kingdom, alone. He was like a tiger looking for its cub. He was attacked by soldiers during the search, but there was no obstacle that could've stopped him at that point. He later invaded the castle and eventually reached the dungeon. He slaughtered everyone who seemed guilty and had a duel with Amir.

"Is this how you treat me, Sepehr? I-I was once the closest person to you, don't forget!" Charges towards him. Sepehr blocked the attack and pushed him away. "Closest person, my foot, you were always planning something or the other thing behind my back. You fought for the duchy even after being gifted a kingdom half the size of our duchy. You are a greedy man. But I never thought you'd be foolish enough to leave a woman like Esmeray?" Listening to what Sepehr said, Amir started laughing. Sepehr got mad at him and launched towards Amir.

Splash! Sepehr's stabs his sword inside Amir's abdomen. "You know nothing. And once the move is made, you'll be heartbroken. A move that you never knew would ever be made by anyone!" He clenched the sword in front of him and walked towards Sepehr, making the wound worse. "She doesn't belong here…" He eventually lost consciousness and fell on the ground.

Sepehr's eyes started welling up with tears, as he vulnerably dropped on his knees to the ground. He then, vulnerably, unchained Esmeray just as the soldiers arrived.. The capital was on fire. Innocent people, who had no idea about anything, evacuated and the troops to conquer Karanlık also evacuated back to Jabal.

Chapter 5

Chrysanthemums

"As I look towards the moon, I ask myself, can I reach there soon? Life is sour like the first drop of lime, that's when I started thinking about turning back time…" I saw my mom sitting on the same swing and singing the same lullaby, she used to sing when I was a kid. She caressed my hair as I was sleeping on her lap. I lifted my head and looked at her; I was angry about the fact that she left me, I couldn't help but stay calm, "Mummy, why did you leave me? Why didn't you tell me you were going to someplace better than this one? You should've taken me with you. Why did you leave me in such a cruel world, why?" Her eyes softened and looked into mine, her voice sweet as a viola flower, "My will to protect your life was greater than to think of my own." I stood up and my head started spinning. I saw things I had never seen before, yet they seemed strangely familiar. A little boy with white hair and a gentle smile, looking at me with the most tender expression.

With so many memories playing in my head, I opened my eyes. Sadira then hugged me tight. I then asked in a weak tone "W… where am I? Where is Sepehr? Where's the army? Why am I here?" I forced myself to get up. "Slow down, your body is still injured…" her tone soft and her touch gentle. Just then, Doctor Demir walked in, "Looks like you're up, Esmeray. And it seems like you don't remember anything." I looked at him with a gaze full of worry. He understood and sighed, "You really are stubborn, aren't you? A perfect match indeed." Sadira sighed as well. She then signalled Demir to tell her everything. "So, let me help you with that. You are in my private clinic, and Sepehr brought you here as you fell unconscious after you were given this…drug." He then showed me a glass bottle with faint yellow liquid in it. "This is a drug used to torture criminals, and if used in large amounts, it can also kill someone almost instantly. But the amount used on your body is moderate…" Sadira then looked away from me and started wiping her tears. Demir walked towards her and hugged her. "The drug has its speciality, that it kills the person no matter how much is used. It may take some time to kill, but it will kill." He continued while hugging Sadira.

My eyebrows raised at the statement. Why don't I feel better after hearing this? Didn't I want to die? Why am I feeling the greed that all humans in the world feel? The greed to live… Why? He then continued, "This drug is used for a criminal to confess their crime, and the dosage used depends on the time given by the justice holder. The judge. It can be dragged for 3 three years or can be done instantly. As for you, you have…7 months to live." I turned my gaze away. "I see, d-does Sepehr know about it?" Demir then nodded a no and replied, "No, he doesn't, he is to be informed about it after he's done dealing with casualties." "Casualties? What casualties?" I looked at him, confused. Demir looked into my eyes and replied with a sigh, "You see, Sepehr happened to see you in that miserable state, and seemed to have been engrossed with anger that led to the whole kingdom to burn. The fire was so strong that it could've even reached the imperial capital." The news I heard was something not hard to take in. But the fact that Sepehr did it for me is making me feel useless… 'Do I even deserve him?' 'Am I worth it?' I looked at Demir and made a request firmly, "Doctor Demir, I don't want Sepehr to know about my nearing death. If something were to happen to me, I shall tell him myself. As this is something inevitable, isn't it?" Demir nodded. Sadira, who was standing beside the bed hugging Demir, broke the hug and approached me and embraced me tightly.

My dreams started getting weird, and I stayed asleep most of the time. Whenever my body was awake, I would obey whatever they asked me to do. Except for the food they served, it was as tasteless as rubber. They told me that I had lost my ability to taste.

As always, I was resting on my bed, but I was lost in thought and was not sleeping, but rather thinking about 'the family'. Until Sadira interrupted my thoughts by knocking on the door. I looked at the door for a while and snapped out of it, "Come in, Sadira." She came inside and asked curiously, "How do you know it's me?" I chuckled to myself and replied, "It's only you who visits me, Sadira." She then smiled softly towards me and sat on the bed beside me. Her voice was gentle as ever. "You actually have a visitor today." "Huh, who is it?" I thought for a while, until my eyes beamed "Is it Sepehr?" Sadira smiled, pushed away from the bed and opened the door. My eyes widened to see a man standing outside the door, dressed elegantly in a crisp white shirt and tailored pants. His silvery hair, now unkempt due to his preoccupation, lay in loose strands around his face. He clutched in his hands a bouquet, the flowers' petals trembling ever so slightly as they reflected his anxious gaze. His eyes, like two pools of molten metal, shone with an inner turmoil, mirroring the intensity of his worry.

He ran towards me and wrapped his arms around me. His voice betrayed his tough exterior and turned hoarse, "I'm glad you're okay, I'm glad nothing serious happened." His grip on me tightened and his tough exterior shattered; something that had never happened before.

After a while, following the conversation between the two of us, Sadira offered Sepehr a chair to sit. Just then, Dr. Demir entered and smiled at Sepehr. He then got back to his stern professional self and started reading out the words inside the papers he held, "Seems like your internal and external wounds have been healed, you are to be discharged tomorrow evening." I smiled at him as the news was something I had waited for in favour of my isolation for a month.

We were happy until Sadira started in a nervous tone, "I'm really happy that your wounds have started healing, but I'm sorry Esmeray, it seems that I can't stay with you anymore." My eyes widened in shock and I asked, "Why? Did I do something wrong that might have upset you?" Her voice shaky as she replied, "It's not that, it's just..." just before she could finish; Sepehr interrupted, "What do you mean 'not stay with you' isn't it that she needs more attention now than before?" she replied to his question with a shaky tone, "I know that, but Demir and I got married and we are going to start a family together." I understood their need for privacy and nodded, "So, that means that you both are husband and wife? I'm glad for the two of you and I hope to see the little one." A soft expression on my face. But after a little while, my facial expression changed, following the thought that I might not live long enough to see their kid.

Sepehr then asked politely, "Is it okay if Esmeray and I stay together?" A longing face, that looked like a cat, waiting for you to serve its meal. He looked straight into my eyes which had something in them. The softness in his gaze made me feel more protected, and a small smile spread across my face.

Demir and Sadira took their leave, giving us some privacy. Sepehr's hand was on my hand; it was larger than mine and quite soft. While my hand was filled with scars because of the recent turmoil. I lifted my head and looked into his eyes. I could feel his gaze softening after looking into mine. "Your eyes have gotten prettier than ever." He stated while gripping my arm tighter. "Why'd you do that?" I interrupted the peaceful interaction between us and went straight to the point. "Do what?" He asked, which brought a slight tension between us. "Why'd burn down the (whole) kingdom?" He smiled gently and replied, "When a stone lifted up from the ground starts hitting another stone that was picked up from a river, the rough edges of the rock start making scratches on the soft stone. As time passes, a spark appears, which later causes a fire that burns the sand below, the very sand where that rock was picked up from." His words felt like a sip of tea, hot but satisfying.

After some time, my head started spinning, and so did everything else around me. Sepehr kept his arm on my shoulder and laid me down on the bed. "You're burning up, sleep tight and rest well." Everything around me started darkening as I closed my eyes to sleep.

A while passed by, and I opened my eyes and felt a wet cloth on my head. I took it off my head, and it smelled like Sepehr. I turned my head towards the right and saw Sepehr sleeping on the chair; his hands were folded and his head dropped down, hanging. My intense stare at him woke him up. "Oh! You're awake, did the cloth dry off?" his tone was urgent, his expression looked tired, but his eyes looked worried. I just gave a soft smile and replied, "No, don't worry, everything is fine and don't push yourself too hard." He then calmed himself down and said, "We're going to stay under the same roof, huh?" I then looked into his eyes with a gaze given by a mother to her child, "We sure are." A smile on Sepehr's face mirrored on my own.

A dream: 'Don't you think you're hiding too much about yourself from Sepehr?' 'For someone who would burn the world for you?' 'The only way to repay him is…' I quickly got up from my sleep and sat up. I kept my hand over my eye and sighed. Suddenly, I saw something that made my brows frown; my hand had gotten a purple patch, it's the result of the drug, and it would slowly start spreading everywhere in my body.

I overslept and had to be woken up. I was then served breakfast, which I had to push down my throat, as it was tasteless. Dr. Demir then entered my room and informed, "Since you're not going to stay at the hospital anymore, you are to be informed about your conditions." He cleared his throat and spoke in a firm tone, "I know you're a strong lady, so I'm certain that you'll bear with it. I'm also very sure that you would bear it to the point where it's unbearable and downplay it. I don't want that happening, I want you to tell Sepehr about it, as it is not something to be taken lightly." I nodded my head and promised, "I shall listen to what you said, Doctor Demir." He smiled at me and continued speaking about my condition till lunchtime.

After lunch, Sepehr was at the hospital to pick me up. He then thanked Doctor Demir and teased him a little as well.

We eventually reached his place and got settled down. Sepehr then walked up to me and spoke in a gentle voice, "Everything is settled, Ms Amani, oh wait Mrs Demir helped me set up everything. If you ever need anything, I'll be in the study. Please don't hesitate to reach out to me, okay?" He took some of my hair in his hand and kissed it. I smiled and replied with the same gentle tone, "I will, don't worry."

Three days passed, I stayed in my room and started writing something in my diary. I've planned on publishing a book; I guess now's my chance to do so. I kept writing for days, until I realised something was off. Sepehr, who is supposedly living under the same roof as me, is nowhere to be seen; it's almost like he has disappeared from his own house. I then pushed myself away from the table and walked towards the study. I stood in front of the door and looked at it for a while and later knocked on it. "Umm, Sepehr, do you have a moment?" I then heard his voice from the other side of the door, firm and tired "Enter!" His voice brought chills down my spine I opened the door and entered; I closed the door behind me and walked towards his desk, which was surrounded by shelves. "Sepehr, why are you all cramped here? I've never seen you leave your study, ever since I came, why?" I asked him with a spiteful inquiry. He kept the papers he held in his hand on the desk and straightened himself up, "Well, it's about work and I've gotten a bit carried away with it. Which is making me lose my sleep and skip some of the meals. I was just agitated to tell you, because you just got discharged and if I get you involved in work so quickly, I would be called the worst." I smiled a bit and said, "Well you know what, it's fine and I've been so bored lately that I wanted to work soon too." His excitement matched the energy of a child, but before that, he confirmed by asking in a gentle voice, "Are you sure?" I then nodded with confidence, "A hundred percent!" He got up from his chair and got me another chair to sit on. He then sat in his place and handed me a pile of papers. I recognised that the kingdom of Odun had gotten into a lot of trouble with us and were plotting something behind our back. I looked at Sepehr, who was working with the other set of papers, about Karanlik. I sighed and asked him gently, "Sepehr, why is Odun trying to cut ties with us?" He then looked at me and replied, "It's that our kingdom has broken the agreement between them. They said they'll ambush during the crown prince's coronation day." My brows frowned, I thought for some while and figured that the plan mentally pictured in my head could also have an eighty percent chance of dying. How can I ever let Sepehr do that part? I looked at Sepehr and said, "I don't think a war is necessary." Sepehr then looked at me, confused and asked in a curious tone. "So, what's the plan?" I looked at him and smiled confidently. I then took a sheet of paper beside him and started explaining the plan to him. After a few minutes,

Sepehr noticed the drops of sweat on me and said in a concerning yet firm tone, "The plan sure is risky, but we don't have much time, the coronation day is tomorrow and I don't want yo-." Just before he could say something, I interrupted, knowing his disagreement, "I don't want the kingdom to go chaotic, I just want every child to live with their family without worrying and hoping they could rely on us." His face didn't look like he agreed to the plan but his voice was confident, "I may not agree to your idea but I guess I have to, as you've turned yourself into a weapon or probably a shield." I smiled at his agreement and dismissed my plan, "Since we don't have much time and the plan must go on. Then I presume that some of your workload is lifted and suggest that you take some rest and regain your strength for the execution of tomorrow's plan."

After a while, I noticed that he didn't seem okay to me, but he never complained about it, so I asked in a concerned tone, "Sepehr, are you okay?" he looked at me, smiled and walked to his room, but didn't reply to my question. I didn't want to push any further and so I went to bed myself.

Well, not every night I get a good night's sleep. That includes this night, I guess it's better not to mention everything, after all, tomorrow is the day we shall proceed with our mission.

A ray of sunlight fell on my eyes, which woke me up from my slumber. I then reminded myself about the mission and got ready. I searched for Sepehr everywhere in his house, but he didn't seem to have been anywhere. I trusted him and didn't continue the search, and left for the kingdom of Odum. I trust him. So, the plan goes this way: I go to the kingdom of Odun and try convincing the king to stop the war. Until then, Sepehr has to bring the king's seal on an agreement of trust.

I feel guilty for involving Sepehr as he has to travel a long distance even though his face looked dull that night.

Eventually, I reached the King's palace and made myself in. Luckily, I passed the guards and eventually reached the throne room. The guards suspected me and took away my weapons, as a 'royal protocol'. I hated it when someone takes my sword, well, it's given to me by a special someone after all.

I cleared my silly thoughts away, took a deep breath and entered the room. I looked at the king, bowed down and spoke in a firm yet respectful tone, "Your highness, it's an honour to be in your presence." He then looked at me with the sight of arrogance and had a stern tone "who are you? And what is that you want from me?" the arrogance in his eyes pissed me off, but I kept calm and answered to his questions respectfully "Your highness, I'm someone who's presence you didn't hope, for I am a warrior from the kingdom of Jabal—" just before I could continue the guards approached me, kicked the back of my legs and got me on my knees. They got on their toes and kept spears around my neck. They even tied my hands behind, making me hard to move. The king had grown quite furious and got up from his throne. He then walked towards me and exclaimed, "You filthy people have never come here to give us any Good News!" "But this time-" a soldier punched me in the face and didn't let me speak. The punches continued, not just my face but my stomach too. I showed no reaction which pissed them off. The beatings continued until the king halted them with his hand, "What do you want from us? Or do you have a death wish?" I looked at his eyes but in a respectful way, so that the plan doesn't go into ruin. I then replied in a firm tone, "I'm not here for war or for further bloodshed, I'm here to bring the words of the king." "Not through the messenger, as they will be coming out from the king himself!" A commanding voice interrupted. It was the king who had raided the castle and had entered the throne room.

Just after I saw Sepehr's face, I felt like all my anger and every other pessimism just disappearing away... But his pale face made me really worried. And I walked towards him after the spears were lifted off my neck. I looked at him with a soft gaze and asked him in a concerned tone, "Sepehr, are you alright? You look pale, are you sick?" he then did the same thing as before, smiled at me and walked towards his majesty. I was really concerned for his well-being and wanted to interfere, but he seemed to have been ignoring me ever since I came to his residence. Is it because I didn't tell him about my condition, or am I being too annoying? Thoughts ran inside my head like horses.

I waited outside the throne room while his majesty had a long conversation with the king of Odun. I asked one of the royal knights about the arrival of the new king himself. One of them looked at me and replied, "His Majesty is still in his youth, he's still productive, and wanted to explore a lot of places since he was a child. He hated the fact that he was the crown prince, but he cared about his people. The reason for the war was also his father's fault. In order to fix his father's mistake, he brought his presence." He seems like a really nice man. Finally, Jabal has a good king.

A few hours passed and the truce was made. Later, a trope went back to the kingdom with the king, and the second trope left a few minutes later. Sepehr and I were in the same trope.

We rode our horses for quite a distance, and just as I thought everything was going peacefully, Sepehr's horse reared toward me.. I fell from Kieran's back to the ground. Then I noticed his horse acting strangely, as if it wanted us to see something. My eyes were blurred because of the fall, but as I saw Sepehr not on her back, I quickly sat on her and she took me somewhere near a forest. Kieran also followed us like a lost puppy. Just a few miles, I saw Sepehr hyperventilating, sweating and unconscious on the ground. I quickly got off and rushed towards him. I then sat beside him and kept his head on my lap; he seemed to have a really high fever. I then picked him up *to find him* really heavy. I somehow took his large body towards my horse and gently laid him down. I then ordered a soldier to inform Dr. Demir to bring his presence to Sepehr's mansion.

A few hours later, we were at the gates, and the security had grown tight. It was because of the King's coronation day. I was in a hurry and I rushed to Sepehr's mansion from a shortcut. After reaching there, I carried him to his room. I then felt a sharp pain around my neck and coughed up blood on my hand. I quickly laid Sepehr down on his bed and washed my hands. Looks like the drug is showing its presence to me. I could care less about it, and immediately tended to Sepehr's basic needs. Just after a while, Sadira and Demir arrived at the mansion. He did a quick examination and explained in a calm tone, "He seemed to have fatigue and overworked himself for the past days." He then handed a herbal tea that could give relief to the body. Just as I took the bottle, Sadira observed the stiffness of my actions and asked in a stern tone, "Did you hurt yourself during the mission?" I then nodded my head in a confused way and said "No, why'd you ask?" She then held my left arm and exclaimed in a tone of anger, "Then why does your face look pale?" I didn't reply because a doctor knows their field better. Sadira then did a quick check-up and found out that I had a few bruises on my body and mild cuts on my neck. She then wrapped a bandage around my neck after applying some ointment. I thanked her and asked the maids to bring in some tea for them. Demir then explained in a stern way, "Esmeray, looks like your conditions have gone far worse than I thought. But as you are a warrior your health is declining drastically. I suggest that you reduce or completely remove your presence at the battlefield Your platelets have given up; it's going to be hard to stop you from bleeding." His words didn't worry me much and my mind was stuck on Sepehr's well-being. Demir observed it and suggested that they took their leave. He took a final glance towards Sepehr and took his leave.

Just after they left, I was on Sepehr's side the whole time. A letter from the king's palace had arrived, stating our summon to the king's palace the day after tomorrow. I then let a big sigh out and heard a faint, weak tone, "What's with the long sigh?" I turned towards Sepehr and saw that he had woken up. He then gave a soft smile and said, "Now that I've seen you okay, I can rest in peace." My eyes then opened up in shock and asked him in a really shocked tone, "I-In what way?" he then laughed at me and said, "I've never seen a shocked Esmeray before, besides I've never seen Esmeray out of guard before." I then cleared my throat and reminded him in a stern tone, "Sepehr, Dr. Demir has kept some tea for you, it's better if you drink some. Also, get some rest, it's late." I then left his room and wrote a reply to the king. And walked back into my room.

A sudden loss of balance caused me to fall on my knees, my eyes got blurry and my nose started bleeding. A sharp pain was also felt around my wounds. I then realized what Dr. Demir tried to tell me in Sepehr's room. I then wiped the blood and went to bed. Unfortunately, I couldn't get any sleep since the nose bleed wouldn't stop and I had to work on It for a while and decided to sneak into Sepehr's room and look after him, since he's not fully recovered.

I sneaked into his room to find him asleep. I then sat down on the chair beside his bed and kept watch. Just like that, a few hours passed, and I was sitting on the chair beside his bed. The moonlight's rays were falling on the book I was reading, from the window facing me. While I was reading, I heard a voice, which sounded really attractive, a sound that I didn't want to unhear, it said, "My dark nights are finally being illuminated because of the moonlight. Whose moon is behind it? Is it because of the moon, which belongs to the earth. Or is it because of the moon, which belongs to me?" Just as I heard his voice, my attention was all grabbed by him. His snow-white hair was shining because of the moon's light, which made me let out my thoughts out loud, accidentally "My precious diamond which is shining through the moonlight, shine through all the nights I'm with you." I then closed the book, cleared my throat, and said in a stern tone, "Oh, looks like you've woken up from your slumber. Are you okay, now?" Sepehr then looked right into my eyes and said, "Yes, I woke up, but why did you open the windows of my room? Did you forget what I told you? The windows of the mansion can be done anything but not the one in my room." He then let out a big sigh as I looked into his eyes in concern. "It is because Demir said so, how am I supposed to ignore a doctor's words?" He then gave a minute's pause and said in a tone of agreement, "Ok, fine, I won't force you, but you didn't go to sleep, are you okay?" I then looked at him with a soft smile and said, "I'm not really tired." I then kept the book I was reading aside. Just after that Sepehr asked in a tone that was loud but sounded upset, "What happened to your neck? Who bruised the pretty face of yours? Tell me! Was it the people of Odun or…" I had my hand on my neck, which was bandaged, "Oh, you mean this? These are just scratches which got inflicted on my throat through those spears. And the bruise on my face must've been because of the first stage torture." Sepehr then got up from his bed and looked right into my eyes with anger and said, "I told not to take on something that's too risky, BUT WHAT DID YOU SAY? 'Oh my Sepehr, I don't want you to die' I DON'T CARE! I got anger flared upon me and said, Oh yeah? If you REALLY do care so much about me, why didn't you think about my situation in your absence?" His eyes widened in shock. He then approached me and against the backdrop of the darkened room, he and I stood illuminated by the soft light of the moon streaming through the window. Our forms were silhouetted by the silvery glow of the celestial body. He wrapped his arms around me, pulling me closer into a tender embrace. Our lips met in a gentle kiss, and we were lost in our own private world, oblivious to the outside. His warm lips, soft and gentle as then came in contact with mine. The light from above casted a magical aura around us, creating a romantic and intimate atmosphere that was heightened by the shadows on the wall.

And just like that, dawn broke and breakfast was served. The two of us smiled at each other and had long conversations. The day wasn't as eventful as always.

While the day turned almost night, Sepehr asked me, "Hey Esmeray, what would you do if you knew that I was dying?" The pleasant mood just disappeared after he asked that question. "As I had mentioned earlier , I would have nobody in this world. And so, I would do anything for you to get you your cure. Even if it costed me, my life." I then looked out of the window and thought, 'Would he tell me about his illness if he got one, like mine. Or hide it from me just like how I am from him?' I then looked at him and said, "It's already late, let's just go to bed and don't forget we have a meeting at the king's palace tomorrow."

Just like that, the night had gotten darker, and my eyelids started getting heavy. In this way, the night passed, and I had fallen asleep on the chair. Just before I could know it, it was already dawn, the rays of sunlight fell on my eyes, and woke me up from my slumber. Well, my back had started hurting me a lot. Could it be because I slept on the chair? I then got the whiff of a rather redolent fragrance. Which felt like an afternoon during winter, you could get the whiff of cologne during a light snowfall and a tiny hint of burning sensation. Well, it could be because of my recent nosebleed, but I could feel a comforting hug, holding my soul tight. I just didn't want to get up or move away from that position. But my duties didn't let me do so. As I opened my eyes, I saw Sepehr standing right in front of the window, sipping his herbal tea. He slowly turned towards me and said in a calm voice, "Looks like you're awake, my moon." I could then feel my blood reach my cheeks and repeat the word 'my moon'. I then controlled my excitement and said "S-Sepehr! Looks like you've woken up too, also this fragrance, did you place your coat on me when I was asleep?" He then gave a smirk at me and continued reading the document in his hand. I then walked towards him and handed him his coat and reminded him in a soft voice, "Don't forget, we have a meeting with the king today." He then took his coat back. And moved along the room to get ready.

We took our leave on our horses. As we were on our path, I saw small children staring at us in awe. I felt proud, and reminded myself of my dream to be in the parade where the soldiers come back to the kingdom with victory after a conquest. I was so lost in thought, but I heard something really unusual from one of the kids shouting at their friends to look at us while we were passing by, he was repeating this to his friends on and on 'Louis! Emma! Come check this out! Silver sword and the Dark blade are on their way to meet the king. It's a sight you'll never forget, they are together!' Wait a second, 'dark', what's with that nickname? I looked at Sepehr, who was giggling after listening to what those kids told. It made my cheeks red, yet proud.

A few moments later, we reached the King's palace and entered the throne room. After we bowed down to the king, I saw the king bowing back at us, but it's rather intriguing to see the king bow down himself. He then looked at me and said in a respectful tone. "Your Highness, the emperor has requested your presence at the Imperial castle." "WHAT?"

Confidential to Esmeray

Sepehr was given the Karanlik kingdom and was asked to deal with the damage caused by the fire. He has lots to do and repair. But the kingdom had given out results that no one expected.

After he went to the king's palace, he almost lost consciousness while explaining the situation to the king about Odun. He refused to take rest as he thought about Esmeray being in danger. He also noticed the bruises on her face, which he took care of while he had the meeting with the king, whilst their king. He asked him questions that would make someone's heart weak and threatened him every second chance he got. He even drew his sword out, but he was not ignorant and didn't do anything but threaten him.

Chapter 6

Diphylleia Grayi Flower

We were astonished to listen to the king's respectful address to me. The king then escorted us to the meeting room, where only the high levels are allowed to enter. The king then requested us to be seated and got to the point. The king had high status, but he didn't seem arrogant. He had a calming aura around him. He had golden blond hair, which seemed like actual gold when the sunlight had fallen on him, his eyes blue as the sky, wanting to explore and know more. He seemed more like Amir but had a more youthful face. He then spoke in a gentle tone, which didn't even think of hurting an ant, "Empress of the Ecrin Empire has requested your presence at the palace, your highness." I couldn't believe what my ears heard. I then turned towards Sepehr to see his reaction; he seemed rather calm. I then looked at the king in a respectful way and asked, "When exactly am I supposed to be there, your majesty?" he then looked into our eyes with a respectful gaze and replied, "Today, your highness." My eyes widened in shock. I had to go and see the empress today!

I went back to Sepehr's place and packed all of my stuff to leave. The king was noble enough to keep us in his Palace till lunch. And helped us depart.

I was worried as I had no clue even about her name. I sighed and looked at Sepehr. His gentle, cold and soft smile melted my heart like butter, and I had no choice but to show a reassuring smile. We then set off to the empire.

On our way, my back started killing me, it's because of two reasons; firstly, because I slept on the chair in Sepehr's room and lastly because of us riding our horses. Five more hours passed, and we had finally reached the imperial castle.

It was as huge as you could fit thirty times the palace belonging to our king, King Deniz. We were then escorted to the throne room. I wonder if they ever get lost in the palace. Sepher had his cold and composed look on him this whole time; he didn't seem a tiny bit astonished. As expected from a rich man's son. As we entered the throne room, I saw a lady having as white hair as a star and the same eyes as mine. She had an aura that made us show respect to her. Sepehr's white hair looked pale in front of hers. She looked at me and spoke to me in an angelic voice. "Esmeray, darling, you don't have to bow in front of your aunt, get up, my child, you too… Sepehr, was it." My mouth opened after listening to her calling out our names. Also…AUNT? She's, my aunt? She smiled at me and said, "I am your aunt, your mother, my sister, was the crown princess to the throne, but she gave up. So, her child is the heir. You, as of now, are the true emperor of the Ecrin Empire, Esmeray Ece Ecrin." Wait a minute, I- I-I am the emperor? She looked at Sepehr and smiled towards him. "Mr. Burfin lives in you, doesn't he? Sepehr? You look a lot like the grand duke. But your eyes…they are your mother's." He smiled and replied, "You noticed? I'm glad…"

We were then sitting on the dining table, invited for dinner. My brain calmed down after being processed with all the information given to me.

The table was enormous. My aunt kept staring at me, and it was unavoidable. I then looked at Sepehr, who was sitting right beside me. He seemed to have no interest in anything besides eating his dinner. I then looked at my aunt and asked, "Teyze? Is something the matter?" She then looked at me with a smile and said in her usual angelic voice, "Oh my, was I staring at you too much? I had this question…. Have you dyed your hair?" I was confused and answered, "I did not, they're naturally this black. Why'd you ask?" She then smiled and said, "Oh really? Well, usually the Ecrins have bright white hair and my sister, your mother, had the brightest in history. You seem to be the only Ece Ecrin to have black hair. I guess you got it from your dad. But you seem to have our eyes, on top of that, your eyes are quite unique and really pretty." We were having deep conversations about my mother while Sepehr seemed quite pale and paid no mind to us.

We were then appointed our rooms; my aunt smiled at me and said, "We shall prepare a better room for you tomorrow." I got chills when she said that. I then went inside the room...Huge!!! Well, Sepehr seems to be doing better than me. I was given better clothes, but I refused to get new armour and a sword.

While I slept on the bed, I couldn't get myself to sleep, first of all because of the drug running in my body made its presence more noticeable. And the second is the fact that Sepehr was the son of the grand duke of the north.

Time wasn't waiting for me, few days had already passed, and the maids of the castle, had already started treating me like the emperor, but something was off. While breakfast, my aunt seemed quite bothered about something, even Sepehr noticed it. I looked at her and asked her in a curious tone, "Teyze, looks like something is bothering you, may I know what that is?" My aunt seemed shocked upon hearing my question towards her. She gave a gentle smile and said, "The situation has turned quite difficult. You see, the enemy kingdom from the south has been requesting a visit with me, but I'm afraid I might get ambushed by bandits on the way. Also, I've not found any imperial guard who's skilled enough to escort me." I guess I get her point for being afraid, as the previous emperor, my grandfather, died after sustaining an injury during an ambush. I then looked at my aunt and reassured her, "Teyze, don't worry, Sepehr and I will safely guard you the whole journey." Sepeher then looked at me with a shocked expression on his face. But he had no choice but to come with me as he knew that I was a reckless person. Meanwhile, my aunt had a smile wide enough to show us how happy she was, she even appreciated our confidence.

But who knew that her meeting with the king was so early? It was overmorrow ! Meaning, we had to start preparing early for the departure! Time really is not on my side!

And with that, the day arrived. We were in our armours and Kieran seemed to had been getting royal treatment as well, for being the emperor's horse. While we took our leave to the southern kingdom. The path seemed quite peaceful; it didn't seem dangerous at all. Since I was the emperor-to-be, I must not reveal my identity as the ruler yet, and so I went with my aunt as an imperial guard. And of course, our northern duke had to come along with us.

After we reached the kingdom safely, we saw that everything was going great the locals were being nice and the kingdom seemed to be a great place. The only problem is the heat. So, what's bothering the peace between the Ecrins and the Ramils? I questioned myself before noticing how Sepehr seemed bothered about the heat, as he grew up in the northern areas of the empire. While we were on our way to the castle, I thought of comforting Sepehr, by teasing him, and so I asked, "Hey, Sepehr you okay? Seems like you're going to melt away any moment." He then looked directly into my eyes and told in a determined tone, "I'm alright, don't worry". My playful smirk faltered and was replaced by concern. I then looked at him and asked him in a more worried tone this time, "I see that you're not doing good, if you allow me, I'll request my aunt to have you in her carriage." He then looked at me with a smile and said "Don't worry about it now, since we've already reached our destination." He turned front and looked totally focused. The large gate of the castle opened up as soon as we had reached its entrance. As soon as my aunt got down the carriage I ran towards her and whispered in her ear "Teyze, if you don't mind could you ask for a room? Sepehr had just recovered from his fever and he seems pale." My aunt then nodded her head and asked one of the Ramil imperial soldier to request their king for a room for rest. As soon as she commanded that, the king walked down the stairs and said in a tone full of pride, "Your majesty, lady Ecrin, it's been a long time, hasn't it? And of course, a room is prepared for you." My aunt then look at him right in the eye. Her gaze towards him could make anyone get on their knees, as she had the ruler's atmosphere . A quality that was meant to rule. She then said in a tone full of pride yet respect, "I hope we're not forgetting about the difference in our power. And I shall correct you; the room is not for me, it's for my guards. I don't plan on staying here and getting straight to the point, sort everything out, I'm a busy woman." The king then respectfully stretched his hands towards my aunt, held her hand and led his way towards the meeting room.

We, on the other had to deal with the heat. I helped Sepehr to his room and laid him down. The room seemed quite cool, which could help calm the heat inside Sepehr's body.

And because of the intense heat, Sepehr's nose started bleeding. I quickly rushed towards him and handed him a handkerchief. It hurt me inside, seeing him in that state. I wet my kerchief (a different one) and kept it on his head to cool him down,

A few hours passed, and my aunt walked into the room. She seemed to have been quite relieved since the matter had been solved at last. While she was in the meeting, Sepehr seemed to have taken a quick nap and had woken up eventually, after my aunt walked in she stated, "I don't want to spend another minute in this kingdom; let's take our leave now." After listening to my aunt's concern, we quickly took our leave.

On the way, I kept an eye on Sepehr, making sure he was okay. I also noticed that our path was quiet. So quiet that it didn't feel right. I then stopped the whole trope, and just then, an arrow hit one of the soldiers. It was an ambush set by the bandits; we were expecting the whole way. Our trope was close to the Jabal kingdom. Sepehr and I had gotten excited and drawn our swords out, looking at each other with a smile. Sepehr then commanded the soldiers to take my aunt to safety. While we got down from our horses and clashed our swords with them. They seemed to have been tough. It was as if we were fighting a snake with tough scales. I was concerned about Sepehr's well-being and had kept an eye on him while fighting. But he seemed to have been doing better than me.

We kept eliminating each one of them one by one. And gradually the number decreased to two. Our energy had drained out and my speed had gotten slow. I turned towards Sepehr to see if everything was okay, since the last one was fighting against Sepehr. Everything seemed alright until I saw one of them charging towards Sepehr from behind. That trick is unacceptable! My body then moved on its own. I wondered where I had gotten this energy and speed from? Eventually reaching there on time, but since my body had grown too tired, I had no choice but to use my body as a shield. As soon as Sepehr turned back, splash! Blood splattered on his face.

The sword had pierced through my abdomen halfway. I then saw Sepehr killing that man brutally. My eyes then started to grow blurry and I started to lose consciousness. I lost my balance, but before that Sepehr held me, preventing me from falling. My aunt also came running towards me and all I could hear were a muffled 'hang in there' and 'we'll get you through this.' My sight and my hearing started getting faint, "F-forgive me.." I said as I gradually lost my consciousness.

Thoughts started running inside my head, 'I can finally die peacefully without telling Sepehr about the drug. Oh wait, didn't I promise Sepehr that I would get married to him? I guess we were not meant for each other from the beginning. At least I died while protecting Sepehr.'

I saw a girl drowning. I swam towards her and saw that the girl was the young me. I then hugged her tightly from behind, to make her feel comfortable. I whispered in her ear, 'You don't need a popular person as your friend to make new friends. You may not be experienced with friendship, but you'll find people who'll still like you. You respect your seniors, I appreciate that even though the seniors think that you're arrogant. Maybe not now, but be patient, you'll find better people in your life. I know it's hard, I know you want to shout it all out, cry as loud as you can and express everything you have in your heart. I know the first-ever friend you made betrayed you for advantage, she forgot about whatever you did to her. She cried for the one who was there for her when she had everything but not for the one who was there for her when she had nothing. But everyone lives once, and so makes mistakes. Forgive them! You might have lied to them that you had a lot of friends in the past but you were just too inexperienced. But fret not, you will find people. No one supported you since you didn't want any support; instead, you wanted to be someone else's support. And I'm proud of that. They took advantage of it and never asked you about your life. It's because everyone has their own personal life problems that are worse than yours, I'm telling you that everything will be alright. So fight and move on…' A tear fell from the eye of the younger me, and then the adult me turned into bubbles. The sight turned all black until I started hearing people's voices.

Following that, I opened my eyes, and I was alive. My wound was bandaged and the room seemed familiar. Wait a second, I'm back at Sepehr's mansion? Well, I'll slip that fact out as I've been unconscious this whole time. The wound hurts a lot, plus the drug inside my body is acting up; it feels as if someone is stabbing my wound over and over. The noise that was coming from outside got louder. I then clenched my wound tightly and walked towards the door and opened it. I then asked in a weak tone "What's going on out here?" I then saw Sepehr fight with the imperial guards who were guarding the door. He had an unsettling look on his face which would give chills to anybody. His gaze softened as it landed on me. His voice tripped and he said in a soft tone, "E-Esmeray?" he then pushed the guards away, ran towards me and hugged me tight. "Ow, Sepehr be careful, I'm still wounded." I reminded him in a weak tone. He then lifted me up and took me towards the bed again. He then looked into my eyes with a sense of guilt and told me in a concerned tone, "Don't move, you might re-open your wound, I'll go get Dr. Demir." Just after he left the room, my face started turning red. I started blushing because he CCARRIED ME? IN BRIDAL STYLE? Looks like someone likes carrying someone (me!)? While I was lost in thought, Sadira came running and hugged me in tears. "S-Sadira?" I then gave her a soft smile and hugged her. A soft, reassuring tone, "It's all fine now. And I'm back home." She then gave out a small chuckle while crying and said, "Welcome back, your majesty." We then broke our hug and Sadira sat on the chair beside my bed. I then looked into her eyes with a smile on my face and asked, "So, how's life with Dr. Demir? Did you receive the letters I had sent you?" She wiped her tears and replied while having a smile on her face, "It's really fun, I get to learn new things with him. And yes, I received all of them." She then had her cheeky smile and said "Well, your aunt has promoted us to imperial doctors." That's something she didn't exaggerate; I thought she'd give them a whole kingdom as a gift. "You can expect more from my aunt." While we were talking, Dr. Demir knocked on the door and came in after the permission was given. He looked at Sadira, sitting on the chair and said, "Well, looks like you woke up, Sadira here was super afraid to lose you after she saw your pulse drop the other day." Wait a second, I may have misheard it. "Pulse drop? What do you mean?" Demir had his professional tone with him, "Well, after the second surgery, you experienced bradycardia. As day became night and night became morning, your heartbeat got slower and slower that we approximately had a 70% chance of losing you. After your body stopped reacting to stimuli, we started keeping a full eye on you. We lost hope, but Sepehr started getting a bad feeling and insisted on seeing you. We were afraid that he might go into a rampage after finding out about your conditions." After listening to whatever Doctor Demir said, I got a question in mind, I had a confused look on my face until I asked, "A second surgery? But why?" Sadira seemed hesitant to talk about it, and so did Dr. Demir. Sadira then took a deep breath and said, "Well, since your injury was deep, it damaged your reproductive organ, so in order to slow the process of the drug we had to remove your organ. So that means...you won't be able to give birth to a child." I was more than depressed; I don't know how to express that either, I was devastated. Just by looking at my shocked face, Demir and Sadira left my room, knowing I needed some time with my own.

Right after they exited, I saw Sepehr entering my room. I held my wound and stood up. He entered the room and looked right into my eyes. The golden sun's light fell right into his eyes. His grey eyes had turned yellow; they were teary and looked all angry and guilty. I could see myself being afraid and taking a step back until my body touched the bed, in Sepehr's eyes. He looked directly into my eyes and said in a firm, soft tone, "H-how long do plan on hiding stuff from me? Why? Why do you hide stuff from me? Have I not done enough to gain your trust? Wait… What nonsense am I talking, right now? Y-you don't even remember!" Before I could've said something, he left the room and slammed the door. I could see the golden droplet fall from his eye onto the carpet.

I then stood there for a while, trying to figure out the whole situation.

What was I supposed to do? Stay there and do nothing? My heart started getting heavy to endure, and I felt like running away from everything. It's just too hard to handle. So, I took my distressed heart and injured body and ran away from his mansion. I used the curtains, tied them together and rappelled down. I then ran away barefoot on the snow from the mansion and reached the only place that gave me comfort.

I was at my cottage, the only memory I have of my parents. I wanted to scream and cry out all the pain inside me, but my body was too weak to do so. I sat on the swing outside the cottage, which was built while being tied up to the tree. 'Why does it hurt so much? Nothing is happening the way it should've.' I let a long sigh out and saw the condensed steam out of my mouth. I then looked at the sky and saw snowflakes fall. It was a pleasant view. But my eyes started getting blurred, and a warm drop of water fell from my eye and rolled down my cheek. It had been a long time since I've ever cried, and I had forgotten how it felt crying with tears. I bent my head down and leaned my head towards the rope. I closed my eyes while tears rolled down.

I then saw a reflection of me in the mirror, but the opposite. She had white hair and all white clothing. But she looked just like me, because she had the same look in her eyes as me. She kneeled down to get closer to me and started talking to me. She had a harsh tone but soft gaze, "Just how long do you expect to live like this? It's the right time to carry out your plan now. Those people never cared about you. The one who comforted the younger you was YOU. The one who helped you the most was YOU. YOU were the one who had to do everything for yourself when you had no one. Sadira? She cared about a man more than you and left you when you needed her the most. Amir? He joined hands with the girl who ruined your life to take his revenge. Sepehr? Wait, don't tell me you forgot how he bullied you, and he's one of the reasons why you spent your childhood alone. How long do you think you've been like this? You forgot about your childhood because you've been through things that you don't want to forget! It's not love, Esmeray!!! It's your hormones that are deceiving you! 'Love' is just a pretty way of saying 'hormonal imbalance'. Let me ask you one thing, who do you think took care of you in the memory you lost? Tell me!..." Just after the question was asked, I heard Sepehr's voice and opened my eyes and started gasping for air.

He ran towards me and slipped near me. He kneeled in-front of me and looked into my eyes. I gave a small chuckle after seeing him. He gave a small smile but he had guilt all over his face and said, "Esmeray, I'm really sorry, I-I am a coward. I shouldn't have acted like that in front of you. I didn't want to lose you. After hearing whatever Demir said, I was heartbroken and I had to go out to take a breath myself. I-I I don't know what to say..." I then lifted my cold palm and rested it on his cheek. I gave him a soft smile and said, "It's okay Sepehr, I forgive you and I promise to tell you everything from now on. And you are not and never are a coward, okay?" The tears filled in his eyes, fell onto my hand, the cold tears that gave the clear sign of guilt. He looked at me and said, "Now, will you tell me everything?" I nodded my head and told him everything from the nearing death of mine to the inability to give birth to a child. After I told him everything, he hugged me tight. He looked into my eyes and said, "My Esmeray, I may not know how you're feeling but I ask forgiveness for my actions and let's continue living happily, and try looking for a cure for it, okay? About your inability to give birth to a child is a matter I wouldn't care about, as I wouldn't have wanted a child in the first place. So that he doesn't have to suffer the things we had." he then looked at my nose and chuckled. "You look like a rose, because your face has turned all red from the snow." He then put a coat on me. I hugged him tightly and started spilling out, I started brawling and hiccupping. My eyes got blurry and I lost balance. Sepehr caught me in his arms, and I don't remember the rest.

I saw that reflection again, but this time she was covered in blood. She looked at me with eyes filled with guilt and said, "I know you like this one, but deep down you have a sense of hatred towards him too. I know you better than anyone, since I am you. You still hate him for the fact that he was rude to you during the days of learning. Why hide that from him?"

I then slowly started regaining my consciousness. After I opened my eyes, I saw Sepehr sitting on a chair right beside me. He quickly saw me open my eyes and asked, "Esmeray? Are you feeling okay? Does your wound still hurt? Do you still feel your temperature rising?" I then slowly got up and sat on the bed. I looked into his eyes with a soft smile on my face and said, "I'm feeling much better now, and I can go back to my emperor duties, I believe." Dr. Demir then entered the room and stated, "Your conditions worsen, and I shall request you not to get involved in fights anymore." This news made me quite upset and I wanted to oppose that, but before I could say anything, Sepehr had a determined face and replied with a firm tone, "Don't worry, I shall do everything in my power to prevent her from stepping foot on a battlefield."

Those two had a long conversation with each other. My recovery days passed, and we eventually set off to the imperial palace. The road was tough and I had fallen really ill a few times on our way. But reached safely after hours of travelling.

After I returned to the castle my aunt hugged me tightly and lectured me on avoiding getting into trouble. The day of my coronation was set, and the palace was bustling with busy people preparing for the coronation day.

A week later, the heavy crown made up of heavy jewels was set on my head. And the large Empire was set on my shoulders. I sat on the throne, making it clear to everyone that I am the sole owner of that Ecrin empire.

The night of the coronation day, my aunt took me to the imperial library, where all the portraits of the great rulers were kept. Everyone had hair as white as snow except one. It was not a portrait, but a painting. It was a bird feather on a sword stuck in the ground. "Teyze, why is the first frame a painting, instead of a portrait?" I asked in curiosity as I saw the picture up close. She smiled and cleared her throat to begin, "That's a mystery. This painting appeared there after my dad, your grandfather, claimed the throne. And the painting belongs to the founder. He died at a very young age, but had a big impact. Before dying, he said, 'A very peculiar girl would appear, different from the others. Who would conquer the İtibar empire and get killed by her loved one. The one who would change history even after her death. Her signs will be her dreams.' And till this day no one has dared a challenge with the İtibar empire. And it looks like the appearance of the girl is yet to come." We later retreated to our rooms and got ready for bed. My mind was lost in the words said by my aunt.

Two whole months had passed and the nobility were aware of their new emperor. Many meetings about the internal issues were kept and fortunately, the council members were agreeable to my judgements and the Duke of Himmel, Sepehr appreciated my judgement skills. I even realised that the internal war for the dominance was much harder than any other war. Almost every tea party that I've been invited to has been an assassination attempt. But the strong drug in my body does not let any other poison take over my body, almost like I'm possessed by it. My health had been slowly declining, and the purple patches had spread throughout my hand, which forced me to wear gloves, every day.

As I was working late hours at my desk, Sepehr came into my study and sat on the floor. "I'm beat up, the paperwork is too much of a burden to me!" I then continued doing my work but didn't ignore him and replied, "The grand duke must not slack off even without my presence." Sepehr then went quiet for a while and said, "I think I'm an owl." That weird sentence caught me off guard, so I asked him in a curious tone. "Are you, okay? The workload must've made you really exhausted." Sepehr then chuckled a bit and said, "It's because when all the animals slept, I stayed awake admiring the moon." That sentence really did catch me off guard the scratching noise of the pen stopped, and I started blushing. Sepehr then looked energetic and said, "Let's take a break for a while and have fun, shall we? Let's go somewhere?" That request was actually quite good. "I'll ask my aunt about it." The atmosphere then suddenly turned silent. To break this awkward silence, I looked at Sepehr and said, "Sepehr, I love you a lot, but there's a small, a tiny part of me that still upsets me about you." Sepehr's expression changed, he then tried smiling and said, "Well, would you look at the time? I sure am feeling exhausted, maybe let's plan for our trip with your aunt early in the morning." He then left the room after saying that.

Confidential to Esmeray

After Esmeary got injured, Sepehr immediately got on the carriage and took her to the nearest kingdom, **Jabal.** He took her to his mansion and got her treated, as he had called Dr. Demir and Sadira.

While Esmeray stayed unconscious for three weeks, Sepehr went to the bandits' (The ones who attacked them that day) headquarters. He then removed their names from the Bandit's book by finishing off their group. (Bandit book: it's a book given to the nobility and merchants to be aware of such bandits.)

Sepehr was eavesdropping behind the door during the conversation between Demir and Esmeray, hence, he figured that something about her was off and felt guilty about it.

After Esmeray ran away, Sepehr regretted his actions and started looking for her everywhere until his ears froze and the water in his eyes froze.

After Esmeray told Serpehr that she was still upset about him. He went outside the study and leaned towards the door. He was devastated after hearing her words. After everything he's sacrificed for her. He kept tearing, yet he kept a smile on his face while hiding the sadness within him. "She's lost her memories, so of course she doesn't know what I've done for her." He portrayed as though he's not affected by Esmeray's words, but deep down, he kept those words in his heart, written on stone. Which cut him every single day.

He also had a dream about an old incident which happened when they were young. It was about the surprise attack that was done on Esmeray and had gotten seriously injured. But the fact that Sepehr's injuries were worse than hers was forgotten by her. He lost one of his internal organs while protecting her. "We both are even now, are we?"

Chapter 7

Droghego

It's been so long since I've spent time with Sepehr. The wind in this place is so fresh, the salty breeze and the sunsets were perfect for just the two of us. Although I'm all flustered, my face has turned all red. Staying with Sepehr all alone is making me stumble over wrong words out of my mouth.

A few days ago, just as Sepehr told me, I begged my aunt to give us a few days as vacation. She gave us a condition to finish our work within the time period. We worked day and night without rest, and eventually my aunt agreed to it. Before leaving, we made a plan on staying in certain places for the time period given. We were given 91 days in that we chose 7 places. We planned on staying in each place for 13 days. Calculations done by our perfect Sepehr. And those 6 out of 7 places were unique, because of their names not being changed after being conquered. It was because they were beautiful.

First was Shamo, a place known for its scorching desert. Second was Kosetsu, a place known for its beautiful snowfall. Third was Pantai, a place known for its clear beach. Fourth was Schulucht, a place known for its beautiful valley. Fifth was the place where Sepehr spent his childhood, Himmel, a place known for its beautiful sky. We also thought of going to the place where I was born since I spent my childhood in a different place than my birthplace, Qamar, a place known for its moon sightings. And last but not least, we chose to stay in Jabal.

Right now, we're spending our tenth afternoon at Pantai. We were sitting on the sand admiring the sunset. Sepehr looked at me with a smile and started teasing me with a gentle tone, "Hey Esmeray, are you going to sweat a whole ocean now because of the sun, like you did at Shamo? Or turn your face as red as a rose because of the wind, like you did at Kosetsu?" I then looked into Sepehr's eyes and said in the same tone he spoke to me, "Sweat? Turn red? Nope, nothing is going to happen. I've already embarrassed myself a lot in front of you. Besides the sun's not so hot and the breeze is not so cold either, everything is perfect, and you are the reason." Sepehr seemed impressed since I stood up for his joke for the first time and used a phrase that flattered him as well.

The scene reminded me of that day, when Sepehr yelled at me for hiding things from him. Orange sunset made Sepehr's eyes look gold, he seemed so precious at the moment, that I didn't want to take my eyes off of him and I bet Sepehr saw something in me too, since he too didn't try breaking the stare between us. The only difference from that day is that I don't want to stop looking at him, and that day I wanted to gouge my eyes out. I wanted this moment to never end. His eyes were filled with life. And deep down, I felt as if I knew those eyes. As if those eyes were the reason I'm living today. Wait, the reason I'm alive today?

Just as Dr. Demir said; my health was aggravating every day because of the drug. Every night as the moonlight cast through the window, it shines across my face. And when I looked into Sepehr's eyes, I saw my eyes glitter like gems, through the moonlight but masking the pain inside of me. I keeled on the ground, hunched slightly over, trying to escape the pain. Clenched in my hands is my shirt, which I've gripped tightly, as if it's the only thing keeping me from breaking apart. I could feel the cool yet warm tears running down my cheek, but I didn't wipe them away. I could feel a sudden warmth and comfort from behind. It's Sepehr trying to comfort me through the pain. It felt like the warmth of the sun during winter. His body brought apricity in me. He stayed with me the whole night like a shadow. Trying to guard me from any danger he sensed.

The time we spent together went by like a stream of water. The valley in Schulucht was so beautiful. And the time spent there was unforgettable. The way Sepehr tried to cook their traditional food but ended up burning it. The locals over there were really kind. They helped Sepehr clean up the mess and helped him cook again.

Our trip to Himmel turned out pretty good, too. Sepehr took me to his mansion, where he spent his childhood. It was larger than the one he owns at Jabal. Well, it can be expected since his father was the grand duke. No wonder he was so nonchalant at the castle. Right now, his mansion was nothing but abandoned. So, I looked at Sepehr in the eye and asked, "Tell me Sepehr, would you listen to my suggestion?" Sepehr had a smile on his face and said, "Go ahead, I'm all ears." I then looked at the beautiful carved ceiling and said, "Why not turn this beautiful mansion into a museum?" It could be a symbol of peace between my grandfather and your father?

Well, the look on his face was rather hard to understand. His silver eyes looked at me, while his head was all around the mansion. "The idea is not…bad, then that means my father's collections won't go to waste?" He gave a gentle smile at me when he spoke those words.

We then walked up the stairs and there hung two huge paintings on the wall. "Sepehr, what are these two paintings about?" Sepehr's hands trembled a bit, but he then pulled the white sheet that was covering the painting. He pulled out the first one and there I saw the family painting of the Burfin family. "Sepehr is this…" "My family," he trembled as he said that. He pointed at a handsome man who might've been in his 30s, he had red hair just like a rose. "This is my father, he was a gentle yet cold person. It depended on the people he met; my father would even stand raising his head in front of the imperial family, if any of them meddled with his family." He had a proud look on his face as he described his father. His finger then shifted to a lady who was dressed elegantly and had the same white hair as Sepehr. She looked so beautiful and she had beautiful blue eyes which looked like the ocean. "This…this is my mother; she was as gentle as a flower and as fragile as glass. My father loved her wholeheartedly and handled her with care, as he thought she might break any moment. She always rubbed my tears whenever I hurt myself after training and gave me a gentle kiss on my forehead." He had a smile that brought warmth around the mansion as he spoke about his mother. He then pointed at a boy who might've been 15 or 16 years old. He had red hair just like lord Burfin and eyes like Lady Burfin, Sepehr then clenched his fists and said, "This is my brother; he was the greatest person in my life. Even though he was 10 years older than me, he always took care of me without even letting a sigh out. He was my world back then." He then walked towards the second painting and saw 3 young men and a young lady standing. "Who are these people?" Sepehr looked at me with a smile filled with warmth and said, "This young man right here with blond hair? I thought you'd recognize him, he's Amir. The only friend I had. And the lady here is Amir's sister. She was a kind lady, just like my brother. Since both of them were so alike, they both got engaged together. Wait, they even got married, and I was going to be an uncle, until that dream of mine, shattered." I then looked at him in the eye, kept my hand on his cheek and asked "What happened?" his eyes trembled, but he kept his hand on my hand and rested his face on them , "I- when I came back from training, I saw Amir covered in blood. My mother, my father, my brother and even my pregnant sister-in-law, were all lying on the ground, dead! And what did that insane man do? He laughed; he laughed after seeing my weak body tremble and fall on the ground. I was betrayed by my own brother…" His eyes started trembling and dripping; this was the first time I saw him letting his guard down in front of me. I then walked towards him and hugged him tight. "I hope your future turns out to be better than the unfortunate past you've been through." He then smiled at me and walked closer. His hands were on my waist while his soft, cold lips were in contact with mine. He broke the kiss after some time, so that I won't go out of breath.

After talking to the locals around and staying there for 13 days, we finally came to the place where I never thought I'd visit, my birthplace, Qamar. We walked around the place and had their traditional, delicious food. We then stayed at the place where my mom and dad stayed after fleeing from the imperial capital.

Our last night there, we wrapped our bodies with the same blanket, sat on the ground and planned on sleeping. I then rested my head on his shoulder and told him in a half-tired tone, "Sepehr, I've been writing a diary for quite a while." Sepehr was caressing my hair with his large hands and said, "What about it, Ez?" I got all comfortable and said, "I want you to continue my diary; I want you to write the death I'm going to face and... write how you felt." Sepehr then got even closer so that his warm breath could be felt. He then kept his large warm hand on my head and said, "Ez, you don't have to worry about it, just get some sleep. I'm worried since you've been quite nonchalant about your health lately." And just after he said that, I rested my head into his chest and eventually started falling asleep. I could hear his heartbeat and trembling voice, as he mumbled while resting his face on my head, "Please don't leave me. I don't want to lose someone I love again. Even though you told me that you hated me for the fact that I broke your mother's necklace. I had no choice, it contained 'poison'... Please stay with me. Stay with your aunt, who lost her husband in an accident. Stay with your aunt, who lost her unborn child after that accident. Stay for the Sadira who's about to start a family with her loved one. Stay for the lonely Sepehr, who lost everything he ever had." I don't want to cry right now, or I'll be caught for not being asleep. But his words, his words, the way he said them, are making me cry. No, my soul's bleeding right now. The thought that I would lose my life without caring about the people I love. I'm so evil.

After spending 13 days in Qamar, we eventually reached the place where everything started, Jabal. 'Knock knock.' Sepehr knocked on the door of a house. Dr. Demir then opened the door. His face started shining after looking at us, and he pointed the way inside in a humble way. "Welcome Sepehr, Welcome lady Esmeray, please make yourselves at home. After we entered and sat on the couch. We realised their house seemed pretty big on the inside, compared to the outside. It had a warm atmosphere around it. Sadira, whose stomach had a bump, came from her room while holding her belly. I stood up from the couch, walked towards her and hugged her tight. "How's our mom to be?" She gave out a gentle smile and spoke in the sweetest voice I've ever heard, "I'm doing great, how was your trip with Sepehr?" I gave a nod with a smile on my face. Which meant that I had a lot of fun. "I know that she's going to be the best combination of the two of you." I looked at Sadira and Dr. Demir while saying that. Sadira's ears then flushed red and said, "h…how do you know if it's a girl or a boy?" I then chuckled at her reaction and Sepehr too started teasing the two of them, "Oh, don't you know that my Ez over here has built up mana after receiving the drug in her body. It means, she could feel the gender and the appearance within her." Seriously, Sepehr? You didn't have to go so far. Mana? Where did you catch on to these things?? Is it the butler? Or even worse, my aunt? Although the vacation was getting shorter, the fun we had together was unforgettable.

The last day of our vacation had arrived, and the carriage was waiting for us, but Sepehr didn't want to go. He held Dr. Demir tight and didn't leave him at all. "Now, now Sepehr, we are to leave or else my aunt will make us sit under stacks of affairs she left for us." Sepehr then nodded his head and started complaining like a kid. "No no no! I don't want to go back there. Your aunt she, she'll eat me alive. Please let me stay here a bit longer." He acted like a kid who didn't want to go to training on a cold day. Yet I dragged him to the carriage, bid our goodbyes to Sadira and Demir , oh wait, also the little one, and eventually left the place.

It was quite a trip that I wish to never forget. After coming back, I got quite the scolding from my aunt and had to work overtime. A few months later, I found something that I didn't expect. A war between the Ecerin empire and İtibar empire. Half of the empire's places were conquered by Sepehr's father. 'As for the İtibar empire, the people over there are quite the people. The men cheat all day, and drink all night. While the women were all' hmmm…this report is quite dark. The ruler himself is a greedy person. Then, of course, the citizens won't be right, as the rulers are in the wrong themselves. They're ruining the name of the empire. İtibar, meaning 'dignity', which they are not saving. I have a feeling that the whole kingdom is in the grasps of 'the family'.

The report given by Zeki , who's currently working as our spy, in the northern empire is not satisfying at all. As the Acting Empress of the empire of Ecrin, I Esmeray Ece Ecrin shall be a member of this war.

"What! No way I'm not sending you on a battlefield this time. Did you forget what happened to you when you fought last time?" my aunt looked into my eyes with a furious look as if the ocean in her eyes had been hit with a storm. I then gave a gentle smile and said nonchalantly, "Nothing that serious happened?" "You! Nothing serious, eh?" I saw the lightning in her eye right now. "Yes, nothing serious." "You lost the ability to give birth, now if you go out on a battlefield this time, you will lose the ability to breathe." Gosh, that was mean. But her words weren't wrong. "Anyways, I still have to go to the battle in order to prove the founder's words right," I told her with a tone full of determination.

Her face then darkened. "So, you're telling me that this is the only way?" I then nodded to what my aunt asked. After an hour of explanation, my aunt finally agreed but was not really happy with the plan. All the soldiers were being trained every day for the war and Sepehr took the initiative to lead the army. While I held the meeting with the kings of the empire.

On the meeting day, the king of Odun kingdom started boasting about his growing economy while the others boasted about their achievements. King Deniz, the king of Jabal smiled gently while listening to their achievements. The kings were informed of my presence as I entered. I could see the face of the Odun kingdom's ruler turn pale (whilst every meeting I've held so far. He's probably still guilty of his actions.) I handed everyone the piece of document I prepared for them and started the meeting.

Days were passing by and the days of war were getting closer.

There was one day left for the battle. As time ticked, my palms started sweating. I walked through the corridors with a restless mind. In order to bring the truth, I must do something outrageous. As that 'outrageous' thing is…well, outrageous. I must be prepared for everything. I then barged into Sepehr's room and said in a breathless tone, "We need to talk." He then woke up from his sleep, through the noise of the loud door, he pointed at the bed, asking me to sit beside him. I then walked towards the bed and sat beside him. "Sepehr, I want to talk about time with you." Sepehr looked at me in a tired gaze and said, "What nonsense are you trying to say in the middle of the night. Go back to sleep." That's what he said and quickly slept on my shoulder. I then caressed his silver hair gently, tears started falling out of my eyes while I looked at his beautiful face clearly and said "I love you, Sepehr." '

'As morning came up, I divided all the people into troupes and explained the whole plan to them. We both were in the same troupe, and I intentionally did that.

After we arrived at the battlefield, we set our camps as this war would last days. And just like I anticipated, they did last not just days but three months. The Ecerin's had the upper hand but they were quite tough and had good tactical skills. On the last day, something really devastating happened. And that was the cruellest thing ever done to me.

On the last day of battle, the enemy side wore masks and hid their faces; they also wore black clothes in the snow. It was cold and their clothes were annoying. We cut them down with our swords. Like any other obstacle.

Just then, a person attacked me, and that person seemed really good. The gender was unknown, but they were really good. I had a smile on my face, since I didn't had fun for a long time.

But it ended quickly. I then quickly pierced my sword into their chest. While their sword also touched my chest, but was so gentle that it only went through my armour and clothes. That blow wasn't weak, but skilled. I then realized something and my face turned all pale. The battle around me came to an end. But I stood there with the injured person, as I quickly broke their mask to see their face. I could no longer stand on my two feet after looking at the person behind the mask. I collapsed to the ground in sync with the injured person. She had beautiful blue eyes, and tears fell out of them. Her lips made beautiful arcs as blood came out of her mouth, too. She then closed her eyes, making her smile even prettier and fell on the ground. I then kept her body on my lap and started nodding my head out of disagreement. "Esmeray! You, you're heavily injured and it's my fault... Hang in there, hang in there. I'll get you through this pain." She opened her mouth and spoke, "Sepehr…I…I want you to…convey…these words…to some…people." I was worried my eyes started getting blurred because of the tears and I spoke to her in the gentlest yet urgent tone. "Shhhh, don't waste your energy, you'll overcome this, okay? Someone, quickly get the physician!" Her warm hand was kept on my cheeks "Why did you do this?" Tears fall of my eyes as I looked into her eyes. She then smiled at me and spoke with all the energy she had left. "I want you… to convey… the messages… written in my diary. I did this… because…it's the only way…to save you…." I looked into her eyes as she said them until it brought her back "I…I don't want to die…I …I just...want to reveal the truth...It was a selfish act...I...I can't handle the pain...anymore...it hurts...I must apologize for my actions...S-Sepher I...it was selfish of me...I apologize...for not thinking about you...this...this is the best death... I could've asked for...for-forgive me Sepehr..."

And that's how she broke her promise in the worst way possible. Making me her killer, making me regret my life. I have blood in my hands that I can never wash away.

> *'The rain which brought back the petal's life eventually became the storm which destroyed it.'*

This was the saddest victory, where the empress of the empire and the moon to my world disappeared. Just like she said, I went to everyone whom she told me to give the letters to.

First, I went to Sadira's house and informed her about the tragic death of her best friend. She was really upset, she was quite weak too, because she's facing the aftereffects of childbirth. She gave birth to a healthy baby girl just as Esmeray had predicted. She then slowly opened the sheet of paper and started crying after reading the content.

Dear Sadira,

My dearest friend, the only one I had. I wish you good health and a happy life. Just so you know that, when you get a child, I'm sure that you're going to be a mother of a daughter. I also wish you and Demir a happy life.

Sadira, in my absence, please live the way you did back then when I didn't exist in your life. The palace's food is really delicious, but I miss the porridge you cooked for me. Your brown hair in the wind looked like the blossomed trees I saw in Kosetsu. I didn't see them but I've heard they are really beautiful. Your eyes look like the crystal my mother always wore in her right hand, the Amethyst gem. They always shone at me even if mine didn't. I wish that the shine in your eyes lasts for an eternity.

Also, tell your dearest husband that I thank him for everything he has done for me, and always treating me like his own sister. Even if he had a stern look on his face, I could always see his smile and his hidden relief. I could also notice the tense face he had when he saw his friend unconscious on the bed. Please accept my gift as a token of gratitude, even if it's too small.

Also, I'm sorry for troubling you.

your friend Esmeray Ece Ecrin.]

I then handed them the golden envelope, sealed by the emperor herself. They had a shocked face and exclaimed to each other. "A mansion in the capital, a hospital built in our name and free education for our child!" I chuckled and walked away with tears in my eyes.

I then reached the palace and handed Esmeray's aunt the envelope. She then opened the letter and started reading the letter.

Dear, aunt

With you by my side this year, I never felt the absence of my mother. You always treated me like your own. You never tried to get your true feelings with the plans I used to make. Your white hair, shone as bright as the sun, guiding me. Your blue eyes looked into mine with affection every time they reached me. You also accepted Sepehr, even though you looked at him with slight anger, like a father to his son-in-law for taking his daughter away.

I love you as much as I love my mother.

Your niece

Esmeray Ece Ecrin

She had tears in her ears. I then handed her the blue envelope I wanted to give her. She read the content in the letter and burned the letter. "I'm sorry Sepehr, but Esmeray has another plan. And she doesn't want you to quit your work as the Grand Duke." It's not like I want to stay as the duke, but without arguing, I took my heavy heart and went to a place where I thought I would go to after I finished giving the letters.

Under the tree, a swing was hung and under that tree was the Esmeray I killed with my own two hands, buried under the soil. I leaned towards the tree and started reading the letter she left me.

My dear Sepehr,

I caused you the worst pain. I asked you to kill me with your hands. Don't blame yourself for that. Hate me instead. I broke the promise I made with you, forgive me, since I have something, I want to prove. But I want you to find that out yourself. It's something I won't regret dying. It was the best death I could ever ask for. The death I longed for. Getting killed by the hands of my lover.

Your beautiful silver hair, just like the snow, they were cold but brought warmth into my heart every time I looked at them. A familiar feeling I always got whenever I saw you. The ocean I was drowning in was no longer dark after you told me that you liked me, the cold breeze turned into warm hugs and all the pain I suffered turned into memories. The eyes filled with affection for me, the warmth I had never received, even from my own father. The eyes that pierced my soul the day you got angry. The eyes that would kill anyone, even if they were your close ones. The eyes that I fell for. Belonged to the one I love the most in the world. I love you with my whole heart, Sepehr.

Your troublemaker

Esmeray Ece Ecrin

I crumbled the letter in my hands, held it tight against my chest. Let the tears roll down my cheek which I held for so long. I cried my heart out, screamed my lungs out and held the letter in my hands as if my life depended on it.

You wanted to know how I felt when you died, don't you? The darkness in my heart spread, just like the way your blood turned the white snow red. The river of life in me dried up just like the last tear you shed for me after apologising. Your eyes which shone just like the Aquamarine gem, the way their light was taken away. That's how the light of my life faded away, too. Will I ever live happily? I don't want to bear the sin of killing you, even though it was what you wanted. I promise to come and water your grave every now and then. Keep different types of flowers and tell you a lot about them. Esmeray, even though you stole my heart and broke it, I'll still love you with the shattered pieces in my hands as they hurt me.

I picked up the pen to finish the beautiful writing you wrote:

Once upon a time, lived a girl who lost her family at the age of 5. She was then raised by an orphan who was the same age as her. She got bullied by a boy named Sepehr. She lost her most precious thing in the world. She even lost the memory of the orphan who raised her. She faced death at the age of 14. She didn't have any friends for 21 years. She went on battles with the guy she hated. She was proposed to by the one she hated. But the one she always hated became the most loved person in her life. She loved her with all her heart. That she almost sacrificed herself. She even promised that she'd stay with him. But she betrayed him and made her lover take her life. This is how I conclude her story. A lady loved by some and hated by many will receive more hate in the future because of me. I was an idiot who was blinded by love. And my blindness has no cure. The lady I mentioned is Esmeray Ece Ecrin, the former empress of the Ece Ecrin Empire. The one whom the founder spoke about on his deathbed. I conclude my story on 'The Doleful Petal.'

The Duo Petal

Three years passed; Sepehr was watering the grave. He then heard a familiar voice, "So, she died, huh? She got the death she wished for?" Sepehr then turned back to get a glimpse of someone he didn't expect to see, "Amir! How dare you show your filthy face in front of me? H-How are you still alive?" He's tall, with his long blonde hair flowing down his shoulders. His striking blue eyes seemed to contain the very essence of the night sky within them. A single, circular burn mark marred his otherwise handsome face, a stark contrast to the smoothness of his skin. But it was the grief etched into Sepehr's features that drew his attention, the memories of Esmeray casting a shadow over Amir's eyes and leaving a bitter sweetness in the air. Amir stood there, stunned, as if he had seen a ghost. Or maybe he did…he saw dark black hair like the void, behind the tree, but not the person.

He then got his consciousness back as he turned back towards Sepehr, "You're the one who killed her. Why are you blaming me?" He growled. Sepehr's gaze on Amir got darker and his tone angrier. "What? You clearly used the drug on her to kill her, and yet you blame me. Are you going to blame me for killing my kin, too?" Amir had a confused look on his face, and he looked at Sepehr and said with a smile, the same smile he had when Sepehr thought he saw on his face in front of his dead sister, and raised both of his hands as surrender, "What did you just say? I didn't do anything…"